TALL, DARK & DELICIOUS

Edited By

MARCUS ANTHONY

Herndon, VA

Published in the United States by STARbooks Press

PO Box 711612, Herndon, VA 20171

Many thanks to graphic artist John Nail for the cover design. Mr. Nail may be reached at: tojonail@bellsouth.net.

Printed in the United States

Herndon, VA

Contents

NO OFFICIAL GUIDEBOOK FOR PUNTA MITA
By Derrick Della Giorgia

When I dumped Esmeralda and Paco and jumped in the cab with Manuel, I left them without any remorse. They stood there mute, more disappointed than tired and looked at each other implying that they needed to go back to the hotel; the party continued somewhere else, but they were not invited. I simply hailed the cab, avoided the water puddles – which were omnipresent in the uneven streets of Puerto Vallarta, smiled with satisfaction at the black stains all over my white cargo pants, contracted my toes to keep my flip flops glued to the soles of my feet, and once my head was resting on the back seat of the old Sedan, fixed my balls before Manuel got in.

"Punta Mita, *por favor*." Manuel answered our cabbie's question and lit a Viceroy he extracted from the bag – a Burberry purse he stubbornly and quite haughtily claimed as unisex – he wore clumped between his right arm and the side of his thorax as a synthetic extension of his ripped body. He would tell you the collection that bag belonged to, the percentage of leather and suede it was made of, the exact name of the color – it wasn't beige but camel, the similar models on the market and the perfect outfit to wear it with, but he refused to be serious about his age or anything that concerned his sentimental life. "I am twenty-one or twenty-five, what does it matter?" "A boyfriend? I'm not sure I can grasp the meaning of that term …" "All I know about you is that you are on vacation and looking for the hottest guy to hook up with. Why do you need to know more about me? I am here to have fun." Some protective secrecy was more than expected and justified considering I had met him only three hours earlier at a Saturday night pool party, nevertheless his was definitely a lifestyle, a modus operandi, a state of mind. As we left the state of Jalisco and entered Nayarit, the fact that I had abandoned Pace and Esmeralda acquired more meaning and hit me for the first time.

"Is it really going to take us forty minutes … that's crazy …" I hadn't seen my friends in two years; it was my second night in Mexico after a fourteen-hour flight; I had had all the sex I wanted back in Madrid … and still no remorse for Paco and Esme. When I saw him, everything else lost importance, and my interest was swept away from the night. Drinking his beer with one foot on a step, dancing to Madonna in a remote area under the palm trees where the bosses of the place gathered, I couldn't help but desiring him, the most violent and absolute way. His enigmatic presence – very masculine and bohemian except for the bag and his expensive brand clothes – almost challenged me, pushed me to explore his evident arrogance and the beautiful red lips that he kept sealed around the neck of the Corona in his right hand.

"He is hot. But he looks too young and inexperienced for me. Nah." Esmeralda commented after I confided to her I wanted him. "Hijo, you just got here. Take some time to relax before jumping on the first adventure." Paco was calmer than Esmeralda and I and professed the easy-life religion, no hurries in this world.

"It's worth it, you will see." Again, very seriously he let me know we had to do that, as if life couldn't be missed that morning. He shut his eyes and rested his right hand above my knee, making me know he was worth it, too. The dawn was about to explode, and the humid perfumed air that his open window trapped almost put me to sleep, too. I slowly got used to the loudness of the sedan motor and the deep bumps our driver didn't care to avoid. The jet lag became sweeter, and I felt as if I was in Wonderland, everything around me out of size or excessively bright and noisy. I enjoyed the car vibrations so much that I almost missed them when the guy would stop for a light.

We were directed north, to the very end of Bahia de Banderas, where "the water and the sky try each other, and you can touch the clouds." It sounded fantastic, but when he talked – and even more now that he had left his flat stomach and his full crotch defenseless and open to my attack – the only thing I longed to touch was his ass and that piece of chest that was granted freedom from his white collar shirt. So far, I had only managed to steal a quick kiss, in the restroom right before opening the door to get out, when we stared at each other a little longer than bearable. "Don't kiss me. I might like it" had been his smart remark and his warning at the same time.

The second time I went to the restroom alone, and it was even more tempting. The guys were wild at that hour and smelled foreign flesh a mile away. The one in the urinal next to mine – they were so small that you rubbed your neighbor's arm as you peed – abandoned his cock to grab mine before I had a chance to complain, be embarrassed or genuinely like it. "*¿Te gusta?*" He gently asked after his fingers were on my most precious appendage. "You are a hot fuck; where are you from? So tall and big." I tried to explain to him I already had a friend, I made home in Madrid, and I was honored to be held like that – the whole conversation happening while my cock, as to contradict everything I was saying, grew harder and bigger as he squeezed with more and more transport. "Your cock is *muy rico;* are you sure you don't wanna come to my house with your friend?" He proposed, and his hand went down to weigh my balls as old women did at the local market before buying fruit or vegetables, and then under my shirt to feel my abs that he described as

3

"*sabrosos,*" with at least a million S's. Mexico was *sabroso* and captivating!

"I really have to go." I forced my erection back into my underwear and ran to Manuel, worried he had noticed my prolonged visit to the toilet. At that point, Paco and Esme had already given up on me and formed their own click with whom they discussed the best restaurant in Puerto Vallarta, the beach to visit and the club that was open on Sundays. All for me, because they loved me to death no matter what I was able to come up with, driven by my unleashed cravings. They had been together for four years, since the year I had gone down to Mexico for my international student exchange.

Manuel's hand woke up before he did and traveled all the way along my thigh to the zipper that didn't seem to be able to stay up that night. His fingers were long, making his hand look a little boyish, but his nails were strong and wide. His skin looked darker in the car. The black made my mouth water. He couldn't be older than eighteen. His eyes looked so innocent despite the intriguing glances he tried to cast. Was he younger than eighteen? He definitely acted like someone my age though, maybe even older. My thoughts raced through those questions, the vegetation around us, my last forty-eight hours, his beautiful face next to me, the oily hands of our driver that had just finished eating his tacos, and the first hard-on since the light had come back to illuminate the sky. He rubbed the area where my cock pushed the most against the cotton of my pants and played with his fingertips once he localized my head, without ever opening his eyes. My mouth started watering, and all the alcohol and the smoke tasted sweeter. I put my hand on his and pressed with him, helping him provoke my pleasure. Then, we past the village of Brucerias – or better the sign that indicated there was a village beyond the net of trees and plants that devoured the muddy road – and he found my balls and their connection to my body.

"We are almost there." He broke the silence between us and my dreams. I didn't know what I was supposed to do, prisoner of my erection and the spasms his fingers kept giving me. "We gotta get ready." He told me and then "¿Señor?" He shouted to Vicente. "You can drop us where that car is turning, right after those palm trees."

The beach was deserted. Miles and miles of virginity in every direction. Everything was of the same color. The water, the sky, the mountains all around the bay, the sand, even the faraway vegetation. Some unnatural hue between discolored grey and brilliant light blue. Only some of the clouds looked white when they were close enough. All the distances wide and unthinkable for someone that had spent his entire twenty-five years between Puerta del Sol and Plaza Callao. It was worth it; it was so worth it that I had magically forgotten all my bad intentions before getting out of the cab. Grabbing him from behind, kissing him on his lips and pushing my tongue into his sweet mouth, sinking my hand up his tight ass and licking his chest. Fucking him on the beach under the uncertain sun that accompanied that day.

"Do you like it?" He took off his shirt and dropped his bag on it, careful not to get sand near it. Then he undid his metal belt and walked out of his pants, accelerating my respiration again. His briefs were emerald green. Bright shiny silk hung defeated on his contracted butt cheeks as he moved, stretched on his butt crack when he bent, pulled to counteract the weight of his balls, protected the head of his cock, slid down the bone lines of his hips.

"I'm speechless." Perhaps it was my head slowing down after the chaos I had forced it through, perhaps it was the resetting sound of the waves flooding a fat strip of sand, perhaps it was his body or his hazelnut eyes, but I felt weak.

"Do you wanna go in the water?" He stretched his arm towards me. Then he walked over and started taking my clothes off and kissing me slowly and softly on my neck.

"I wanna fuck you better." I finally confessed to him once I stood in front of him in my boxer briefs, my toes buried under the still cold sand.

"Who says we can't do both? You know, there is no official guidebook for Punta Mita ..." He pulled me by the elastic of my underwear and took me to the waterline where he kissed me on my lips. He pinned my lower lip with his teeth and licked its inside surface, as I inhaled the fragrance of his skin. Our tongues found their way to dance together, and we tasted that special saliva that formed in shared territory making it impossible to distinguish the provenance. The kiss prolonged itself in time, and instead of dying under the urgency of more complex love to make, it grew stronger and more satisfying as we learned to perfect it. The waves, despite their delicate noise, were powerful and pushed our ankles out of the water in a slow tempo.

"How old are you?" I locked his angelic face into my hands and waited for an answer.

"No official guidebook."

"I love you." The words spilled out of my lungs, without giving me the chance to weigh them. I had been conquered and had surrendered to him. We sat where the waves broke and touched the parts of our bodies that were still dry, smearing the salty water on every inch of our skin. His body was the perfect synthesis between the archaic Indio stamina and an intricate African blend.

"Show me." He lay down, spread his legs and lifted his knees, letting the sea crash against the green silk that barred his inside. With every flood, his balls bounced, and his briefs got darker and floppier. I put my palms on his smooth thighs and directed my mouth underwater, to his asshole. I ate everything that was uncovered, and then I pushed the elastic with my nose, getting a hold of more flesh.

"Take this off!" I wanted to rip that piece of silk off his hips, but he shook his head and blocked my hands.

"No, you have to fuck me like this. There is no fun in entering an open door." He exposed his turgid asshole from the side and ordered me to eat, digging a hole in the sand with his head and rubbing his face on the side of it.

"Gimme more." I pleaded, without success. The salt of the water burned my throat, and I still wanted it to. The more I pushed my tongue into his flesh, the more violent the sea got against me, almost in a race for who was going to fuck him first or better. He gave me his cock, and I accepted it in my mouth, as the water climbed up my back and teased my butt crack.

"Earn more." He suddenly escaped from under my mouth and got on his fours, presenting me the part of his ass I had only admired when he was standing. I quickly pushed the fabric away, bit where I could snap at the most flesh, and then returned with my tongue to his second pulsating heart. I looked around and felt as if we were the only things that cared to be alive in the stillness of that beauty. His ass was ready.

"Sit on it." I told him, more intensely this time.

"Fuck me. My body is made for this." He got up, turned around and dropped his body on my crotch. Slowly, we were becoming part of the beach, our muscles dressed in sand and our hair wet under the breeze. I was on my knees, sitting on my talons and facing the sea or the sky – because they were both there at the same time in the same place. "Enjoy our threesome."

My cock slid inside him without any hesitation, prevailing all obstacles and reaching a depth at which my pleasure was double because both his tunnel and his underwear rubbed my member with every movement. His waist writhed on me, and his hands flattened on my back. It was early in the morning, and the sun descended on us obliquely, spearing our kidneys and our lungs.

"Wait." My mouth was muted by his fingers, and I was out of him, free in the water. "I want him now." He shut his eyes and rested his face on my chest, arching his back to receive the waves. "It is just as strong as I need it." I grabbed his ass again and stealthily threw a finger in him. Then, I put our cocks together and massaged them in the white sea foam floating in the lake formed by our waists. We kissed, and I licked his eyes, studying the notes played by his eye lashes on my tongue.

"I can't take it. I want you for me." I lifted his thighs and dove inside again, enjoying the increased resistance that his asshole applied on my head. We pressed our bodies together until we couldn't get any closer and stopped every time we were about to come. He was convinced that in the water it is easier to control your orgasm and make it last longer because the water lowers the temperature of your groin and reduces the friction. He bit my nipples and searched with his hand for my hole between my feet. He teased it, pressing all around it and dilating it with his thumb and index finger. I felt the water level rising inside me and a sensation of freedom and openness making me lighter.

"Make me come" I begged, and he smiled and nodded.

"If you would have had me in your hotel, you would have forgotten my name before the cum was dry on the sheets. Here instead, our orgasm will be celebrated in your memory forever. Give us your gift, Felipe." He opened his mouth and bit my lips.

"I'm coming ..." The numbing feeling of pleasure extended all over my crotch, invading my asshole and his finger in it. I grabbed his cock and stroked it with both my hands. When my avalanche of semen was speeding down my shaft, I slipped out of his body and inserted my dick in our private lake where I spurted milk underwater, and as in a slow motion movie I watched it floating to his stomach. He came right after me, above the water level, spraying our salty dry faces with his jet.

ONE ON ONE
By Evan Gilbert

I don't handle stress well at all. It keys me up to the point where I feel as if somebody's jabbed a live wire in me. I stay on edge, jumpy, and so short-tempered that I'm apt to cuss you out if you ask me what time it is. And nothing is more stressful for me than finals week.

At the end of the second semester of my freshman year, I thought my head would explode. My major is biochemical engineering, and after five months steadily reviewing formulas and equations, even my dreams were spinning with numbers. So when I walked out of Breyer Hall after handing in the answer sheet for my last exam of the week, I was in dire need of some serious diversion.

I jogged across the Southern Kentucky University campus to the dorms, where I dumped my backpack beside the desk in my room. The building was largely deserted, and the halls echoed with an uncharacteristic and eerie quiet. Most of the residents had taken off, some just for the weekend, the majority for a long summer break. Heavy class loads kept me from working a part-time job through both the fall and spring semesters, and my parents were swamped with debt from having my kid sister's fractured leg treated last year (she'd needed two reconstructive surgeries, and we didn't have enough health insurance to cover everything). As much as I wanted to head back home to Little Rock for a while, there just wasn't any money to get me there. Fortunately, my scholarship covered the cost of room and board through the summer as long as I took at least one class, and I'd signed up for American Lit 101, which would knock off another of the eight Liberal Arts courses I was required to take. And the next Tuesday, I started a little gig at a local Mickey D's flinging burgers and fries, at least through August.

That still left me broke and with nothing to do early on a Friday evening. So I grabbed my basketball and went down to the old outdoor courts behind the dorms, where residents played impromptu games.

The sun had almost set. It was just a big, red-orange ball peeking shyly over the jagged line of green mountains to the west. The late May air was very warm and humid. I was wearing knee-length black mesh shorts and a matching jersey, material designed to help keep the body cool, but the jog from Breyer Hall had left me a bit overheated. I stripped off the jersey, draping it over a shrub.

There were three courts laid almost end-to-end in the narrow strip between the dorms and a dense, seven-foot-tall line of evergreen hedges marking the university's property line. Each court was regulation-size, but the concrete foundations were cracked, and the goalposts were rusting away in spots where the paint had long ago peeled off. There probably hadn't been nets on any of the baskets in a decade, but proximity alone usually kept the courts packed, especially on weekends. Their emptiness now added to my sense of isolation and loneliness.

I crossed the middle court slowly, idly tossing the ball from hand to hand. There was a vague but familiar tingle in my nuts, which made me realize that it had been almost four months since I'd had the opportunity to fuck around with anyone. Hell, it had been two weeks since I'd even jacked off. My sex life was another casualty of my class schedule. Now that I had more free time, I intended to provide my dick with some much-needed attention. Given my present circumstances, however, it sure as hell wouldn't be getting any tonight.

I started doing lay-ups. The moves were slow and easy, too laid back to work up much of a sweat but vigorous enough to drain off some of my tension. When I got tired of lay-ups, I started lobbing the ball at the goal from center court, lazily plodding after the rebounds. The sun slipped out of the sky over the next hour, and darkness gathered quickly. I decided to head back to my room, nuke a frozen dinner, eat, and then watch television until I fell asleep. Slipping back into my jersey, then scooping up the ball, I turned to go – and that's when I saw him.

He was standing under a tree a short distance from the court. The sight of him sent a little jolt of apprehension down my spine. How long had he been there, watching me? Instead of walking off the court, I started casually dribbling the ball, staring back at him, sizing him up. He appeared to be about my age (19), wearing a white T-shirt, red basketball shorts and big white sneakers. He had a slim build but was broad through the shoulders, like me. He was dark-skinned, around six feet tall, and had a narrow, square-shaped head, again like me. But where I have small, flat ears, his were big and stuck out from his head like flaps. He sported a little shaggy 'fro, while my hair was trimmed close to my scalp. His face was in shadow, which was sexy somehow. He seemed to be giving me the same going-over I was giving him.

He moved forward suddenly, walking casually onto the court and allowing me a clearer look at him. That gave me another, stronger jolt, this time in my dick. Not only did he have a fine, lean body, but his face was damned good-looking with its tight, brooding eyes, broad nose, trim black mustache and plump, unsmiling lips. Silently, he raised his hands, palms outward, and I fed him the ball. Dribbling slowly, he started down the court, bouncing lightly on the balls of his feet, his gaze going from me to the goal behind me.

Ah. He wanted a little one-on-one.

I was happy to oblige. Anything would be better than vegetating in my room under a steady stream of reruns. I got squarely in front of him to block his advance, knees flexed, feet spread, arms out slightly to either side. He kept coming, taking his time. He drifted to his left in a wide arc, as if he really thought he could just circle around me. I shifted with him and closed in. When we were face-to-face, he slowed his steps, coming almost to a stop but keeping the ball in motion.

Okay, let's see what you got. I lashed out with my left hand, going for the ball. He spun at the last instant, whipping the ball away before I could even touch it. Putting his back to me, he used his body as a shield as he kept dribbling. I got up on him, reaching around him, hands swatting for a steal.

He stepped back with his right foot, and I figured he was about to punch into me with his hip. It's a common move in basketball when a defender is playing close, one that is intended to get him to back off. The defender doesn't dare give up too much ground since that almost guarantees he'll be giving up some points, as well. So the offensive and defensive players wind up in a duel of hip bumps and feints until one or the other makes a mistake.

Only it wasn't dude's hip that hit me; it was his butt. And his butt didn't just bounce off my hip. It slid, in what seemed like slow oh-so-fucking-good motion, right across my crotch. His rump was narrow but firm, the slender globes brushing teasingly over my starved dick. The feel of his ass made my whole pelvic region twang, and for an instant, my brain went south. I froze in place, trying to tamp down the erotic charge that ripped through me. It gave my opponent the perfect opening to sweep around me and drive in for a lay-up. Instead, he stopped, too, his back to me, dribbling the ball with light, deliberate motions of his right hand.

He glanced over his shoulder at me, so close now that I could see the color of his eyes – light brown. A tattoo of a yellow and black hornet rode up on the back of his neck, peeking out from the collar of his T-shirt. Was that a school mascot? I'd had no chance to check out any of the university's games this year. Dude had a hard, athletic body. For all I knew, he could play for one of the colleges in town. There was still no smile on his face, but something about the look he gave me was both hungry and inviting. I could feel the heat coming off his body, and that, too, invited me in. The urge to wrap an arm around his waist and press my dick to his ass hit me out of the blue, so strong that I had to grab my cock and squeeze down to keep from getting a full hard-on.

He nodded at me, slyly, as if he knew exactly what I was feeling. I started to give him my name, but before I could open my mouth, dude pivoted abruptly to his left. As he dashed past me, I whipped out my right arm, grabbing for the ball. Rather than using his left arm to block me, he raised it up and away from his body, hand pointing straight out ahead of him. That motion left him open in more ways than one. He managed to shift the ball just out of my reach, however, so that what I grabbed instead was his junk. His balls felt huge, and his dick was semi-hard, giving a solid thump, like a heartbeat, against my palm. It was a fleeting touch. He charged past me, and I turned, chasing him down the court. Brother was fast. He reached the goal well ahead of me and went up in one long, smooth leap, slapping the ball through the naked rim.

He came down, bouncing on his feet, giving me that little sneaky look again. I bobbed my head appreciatively at him, the corners of my mouth turned down, acknowledging his skill. Scooping up the ball, I strutted out to center court, flexing the muscles in my legs and ass big-time, sneaking glances over my shoulder. He followed, his steps relaxed yet thuggishly cocky, his dick flopping loosely beneath the baggy fabric of his basketball shorts while his eyes went up and down my body.

At center court, I turned to him, raising the ball to chest level as I went into a crouch. I tried to ignore the throbbing in my groin. My mind was focused on figuring a way to fake him out, slip past him and make my own drive on the goal. It was dude who pulled the fake, however. He didn't make any fancy moves, didn't even hunker down in a defensive posture. He just raised his hands in a silent, innocent, almost boyish request for the ball.

I'm not entirely stupid. The head on my shoulders said to me, 'Don't fall for those pretty brown eyes, fool. He's just gonna take that ball and score on your ass again.' But then the head between my legs spoke up (actually, it poked up in my shorts), and I handed over the ball as if it were a birthday present.

To my astonishment, he didn't shout "Sucker!" and make a run for the goal. Dude casually turned around, putting that fine backside of his to me again. Bending his knees, he pushed his nice little handful of an ass my way as he began to dribble the ball low. Another invitation, one that I didn't hesitate in accepting. I strolled right up on dude, my crotch smashing against his butt.

He started making little humping motions, pushing back into me the way you would when you're trying to get a defensive player off you. But he was definitely not trying to drive me away. He was positioned so that the crack of his ass was massaging the length of my dick, which was pressed up against my belly. There was no stopping myself now; I got fully, desperately hard.

Dude felt it. The sensation drew a soft, sexy hiss from him as he sucked air in through his teeth. He kept rolling his ass up and down on my cock, all the while bouncing that damn basketball. We were getting a pretty nasty grind on, and my eyes started drifting nervously around the court. If anyone saw us ... But no, it was dark (the university had never installed any artificial lighting back here), and the dorms were practically empty. Even if someone spotted us, the scene could reasonably be interpreted as two guys practicing their offense and defense.

Okay, okay, I didn't believe that for a second. The whole thing was just so fucking hot, and I wasn't about to let common sense make me walk away from it. The ache in my dick worked itself right down into my balls. I had to have more. I stuck the fingers of both hands beneath the waistband of dude's shorts and peeled them down just below his butt. Then I pushed down the front of my shorts, letting my naked dick press up against his exposed valley.

The idea that someone might be watching us was admittedly scary. We could go to jail over what we were doing. I could lose my scholarship, get kicked out of school. My family would be humiliated. But the possibility of being caught also made me even hotter. Too bad I didn't have any condoms on me. If I could suit up, there would be much serious laying of pipe here and now.

And again, dude seemed to read me. As he dribbled with one hand, he fumbled in the front waistband of his shorts with the other. Then I felt him press something into my hand. I knew what the little square tinfoil packet was without even looking. I put a corner of the packet between my teeth and ripped it open.

The condom that I pulled out was already lubricated. I backed up a step, unrolling the condom and slipping it over my thick, hard cock. Dude peered over his shoulder, taking in the sight of my stuff. When his eyes met mine, I could see appreciation mixed with lust there. He stuck his little bare butt even further out. I stepped up to him again, slipped the head of my cock between his cheeks, and started working my way into him.

I didn't want to hurt him. I took it slowly, my hips making tiny thrusts against him, pushing the head of my dick just a little bit deeper into his asshole each time. The tightness of it sucked at me, almost pulling me in. Within a few minutes, I had my entire nine inches in him, and he gave another sibilant cheer.

I started fucking him, in and out, still going slowly. He quickly fell in synch with my rhythm, shoving his ass back to meet my thrusts, still dribbling the basketball from hand to hand. That hot chute opened up completely, and I stopped holding back. My dick rammed away in him, and he grunted loudly each time I plunged in. He clutched the ball in his hands, squeezing it between his palms, too caught up in bouncing his ass to bounce anything else.

I couldn't get enough of this dude. I wanted still more. I wanted to fuck the hell out of his ass, shoot everything I had into him. He seemed just as desperate to take everything, grinding his ass back at me so hard I could barely keep my balance. All those weeks of pent up desire came bubbling up in me like a raging geyser.

I wanted to feel dude's cock. I slipped my hands into the front of his shorts, pulling out his dick. I couldn't see it, but it was hard as bone. I started jacking that piece of meat with the same intensity I was plowing into that muscular little ass of his. Soon, we were both breathing hard, sweat trickling down our necks.

Dude came first. He gave a big, deep grunt and lost control of the ball, which bounced away into the darkness. His asshole clenched on me, and I saw juice spurt into the air in front of him. His asshole clenched again, this time even tighter, and another spurt shot into the air. He shot a third time, and that set me off as I pushed my dick up his ass in one final, sharp thrust. I growled through my teeth, dick jumping rapidly in his butt as I erupted.

Seconds later, the spasms dying down in both our cocks, we stood motionless, catching our breaths, my piece still buried in him. Then, he stepped away, pulling his ass off my dick and tugging up his shorts. He turned to me. There was a look of surprise on his face, as if he couldn't believe what we had just done. I was just as amazed, so much so that I could only stand there with my condom-covered piece hanging down over the front of my shorts. There was something wet on my right hand. I raised my hand and saw that some of dude's cum had dribbled down over my fingers. Impulsively, I licked it off and swallowed it down, savoring the hot, salty taste.

Dude nodded at that. Then he pivoted and ran off the court, disappearing around the corner of the building. I almost yelled for him to wait, almost ran after him. Hell, I was still horny, and I knew I'd be ready for another round in a few minutes. He seemed to be just as lonely and horny as I was. Who knows? Maybe we could be fuck buddies through the summer. Maybe more.

But he was gone. And I didn't even know his name. I had never seen dude before on campus, and there was no guarantee that I ever would again.

Maybe that was a good thing. The memory of him would become a hot wet dream, give me an incentive to get out more and have a little bit of a life.

I peeled off the juice-filled condom and balled it into my fist, then stuffed my cock back into my shorts. I retrieved the basketball and headed for my room. When I got there, I intended to stretch out on my bed, drape that nasty condom across my bare chest, and jack off.

What can I say? I'm a freak.

SEDUCED BY THE PRISONER
By Donald Webb

It's hot and humid, and I'm bored, extremely bored. I'm free, yet I'm a prisoner. This sounds like a dichotomy, I know, but it's because my father is the warden of a minimum-security prison, and we live within the confines of the prison grounds.

My parents are away for the weekend, so I'm stuck at home without wheels. I can't even hitch a ride into town because there's a big sign outside the gate that reads: PRISON AREA – DO NOT PICK UP HITCHHIKERS.

It'll be a relief when I start college in September and move into residence.

I turn on my computer and strip naked. I'm surfing free gay porn sites on the internet, stroking my dick, when the doorbell rings. I pull on a pair of white silk jogging shorts – the kind with splits up the sides – and dash downstairs. There's a man wearing bright orange coveralls, carrying a toolbox, standing on the porch. I've never seen such a young looking prisoner, but he must be over eighteen, or he'd be in juvie. He's probably about six-three, but because of his baggy coveralls, I can't tell what kind of build he has. He scratches his shaved head and stares at me with his charcoal colored eyes.

"Warden home?" he asks.

"No. He's away for the weekend."

He looks me up and down. His eyebrows rise when his gaze fixes on my groin area.

My face flushes when I check my basket and see that my shorts are sticking out like a pitched pup tent, and there's a big wet precum stain covering my clearly visible cock-head.

A perfect set of teeth appear when a big smile spreads across his handsome raw umber colored face.

"I've come to fix the air-conditioner," he says.

I'm not surprised a prisoner has come to do the repairs since it's part of the rehabilitation process. I step aside and let him in the door.

My cock jumps when his hand sweeps across the front of my shorts.

"It's in the basement," I say as I lead the way downstairs.

He follows me into the clammy basement and drops his toolbox in front of the disabled air-conditioner. The temperature seems even higher down here than upstairs. He ignores me and examines the air-conditioner.

"I'll be upstairs if you need me," I say and return to my bedroom.

I'm excited. I can still feel his hand touching my dick. I pull off my shorts, lie on my bed, and stroke my rod. I'm still a virgin, but when I jerk-off, my fantasies always involve men, so I know I'm gay. I close my eyes and pretend he's with me. We're doing things I've seen them doing on the internet.

I spread my legs, spit on my fingers and try to slide one into my chute. It feels good, so I bring my hand to mouth and apply more saliva to my fingers. I can smell my hole on my fingers. I wonder if he smells the same? I'm trying to get two fingers into my chute, but I'm too tight, so I reach into my bedside table and pull out the container of lube I bought last time I was in town. I squirt some on my fingers, and am trying to insert two of them, when he yells, "Can you come down and gimme a hand?"

The top of his coveralls hang below his waist. I can see dark hair peeking out from the cleft between his muscular ass-cheeks. A sweaty sheen covers his velvety smooth back. I want to lean over and lick off the drop of sweat coursing down his spine. When he turns to face me, I can see pubic hair above his coveralls. He smiles and gives me a knowing look, which once again brings hot blood to my cheeks.

"Hold this up while I try to get a bolt into the frame," he says.

He leans over me and works on the bolt while I hang onto the equipment. An erotic male aroma emanating from his body permeates the humid air. He reaches up, over my head, and moves in close. I close my eyes and shudder when his hairy chest rubs against me, and his sweat trickles down my bare back. His hot breath, on my neck, gives me goose bumps.

With nothing to restrain my dick, it stiffens up and slithers out of the wide leg of my shorts into the open air. The piece of equipment slips out of my shaking hands. When I bend over to retrieve it, I can feel his big dick pressing firmly between my ass-mounds. I grind my butt against him.

I'm disappointed when he pulls back and says, "That one's in ... now for the bottom one. Hang on while I slide underneath."

I use a free hand to move my dick back into my shorts into an up-right position. I hope he hasn't noticed. He lies on his back and slides head first under the air-conditioner. His hips bones, and the root of his dick, come into view when his coveralls slide further down his legs. His dick looks like it'll pop out of his coveralls if he moves one more inch. I wish he would. I'd love to see it. His exposed abdominal muscles tense into a perfectly defined six-pack when he moves.

He's driving me crazy. If he doesn't finish soon, I'm going to shoot my load.

"We'll have to change places," he says, bringing me back to reality. "I'm too big to get in far enough."

He stands up and takes over from me. I can feel his cock push against my hip when our sweaty bodies rub together.

I'm all of a dither when I lie on my back, slip under the air-conditioner, and follow his instructions. When the bolt's in place, he gets down onto his stomach next to me, and squeezes his head between my chest and the machine. His hairy armpit is above my face. His masculine aroma drives me crazy. I've never smelled anything like it before. I can't stop myself. I lift my head, push my nose into his pit and take a deep breath. I'm thinking about licking him, but it's too late, he's wriggling out of the confined space.

My heart races with excitement when his hand runs down my chest and over my erection. "Whadda we got here?" he says.

I lie dead still when his hand moves up the leg of my shorts and grips my swollen shaft. "Oh yeah," he says, "nice big piece. I saw it sticking out before."

He pulls down my shorts and tosses them out of the way. I'm completely nude, lying on my back with my head still under the air-conditioner. I can feel his hot breath when he leans over and licks my rod.

24

"Nice and tasty," he says.

I move out from under the air-conditioner. I'm spellbound when he grips my shaft in his fist and sinks my knob into his mouth. I can't believe that at last it's happening to me. He seems too masculine to be a cocksucker, but he is.

Taking his hand off my shaft he grabs my balls and deep-throats my dick, right down to the root. He moans when I place my hands behind his head and fuck his mouth. He pushes my nuts tight up against his nose, and rolls them around in their sensitive sac.

He comes off my dick, sucks my balls into his mouth, and chews on them until I feel like screaming, then he moves between my legs and pushes them up to my chest. Lowering his head, he sniffs my manhole, places his hands on my rump, and lowers his mouth to my anus. He forces the tense tissues apart with his thumbs, and sinks his tongue into my virgin channel. It feels even better than I thought it would. Much better than my fingers.

I'm disappointed when he drops my legs, and moves his tongue up my body, licking the sweat from my chest and armpits. I wish he's go back to my asshole ... it's craving dick. When he's finished with my armpits, he runs his tongue down my leg. I'm flabbergasted when he licks my feet and nibbles on my toes like they're a tasty snack. I've never seen anything like that on the internet.

After removing his coveralls, he rolls onto his abdomen on the basement rug, spreads his legs, and cants his muscular butt.

"I want that big dick up my ass," he says.

I can't believe my ears, but it's obvious by his actions I've heard him correctly. I roll on top of him and try to force my boner into his tight sphincter.

25

"Whoa," he says. "You'll never get that big fucker up my ass without lube."

"I'll get some," I say, and race upstairs for my lube.

When I return, his ass is still in the air waiting for me.

"Use your tongue first," he says as I kneel between his widely spread legs.

When I pry his ass-cheeks apart, his hole, framed by a fringe of black hair, looks much too small for my dick. I lie on my stomach and hesitantly rim my first manhole.

"Put a finger in me," he says.

I squeeze some lube onto my fingers and play with his hole. I can't believe how hot and silky his channel feels when my finger enters him and roots around. He's not as tight as I am, and opens up when I push a second finger in.

"Okay," he says, "Give it to me."

After lubing my rod, I slip him the entire length with one quick thrust. I've never felt anything like it. His hot, smooth chute, grips my naked cock like a second skin. When I push against his butt, trying to get in deeper, he comes to his knees and spreads his legs wide, so I can fuck him doggy style.

"Fuck me," he says. "Fuck me with that big white dick. Fast and deep."

I grab his hips and ram his asshole. The sight of my dick sliding in and out of his tight chute spurs me to greater activity. I'm really jackhammering him when my overloaded nuts explode and my cum floods his inner core.

"Oh yeah, gimme that load," he shouts.

Exhausted, I fall back on the floor struggling to catch my breath. He rolls me over onto my abdomen and orally assaults my virgin ass.

"You gotta tight ass, dude," he moans into my crevice. "You ever been fucked?"

I 'm so turned on I can only shake my head in answer. Even though I've just shot a tremendous load, I'm still horny and ready for his cock. He places a cushion under my hips, spreads my cheeks even further apart, and then resumes rimming me. His hot tongue is driving me crazy. I push my ass back onto his face in an attempt to get more of him into my orifice.

"You be wanting my big black dick up your ass?" he asks.

He's right. I want him in me. I've waited a long time for this moment. I use my hands to spread my cheeks. "Please, fuck me," I say. "I want it."

He takes his time dilating me with his fingers – using plenty of lube, and then he moves between my legs and places his dick-head at the entrance to my chute. I whimper in pain when he breaches my tight orifice. He pauses for a while, and then, when I relax, I feel his dick glide into me. For the first time in my life, I have a cock in me, and the feeling is incredible.

I squeeze his rod with my internal muscles and push back against him.

"Fuck me," I say.

He is quick to obey. He pounds in and out of my tight channel, stimulating feelings that have never before been aroused. His thrusts become faster and faster causing my ass-cheeks to quiver when his hips slap into them. He nibbles on my ear and grunts loudly when he deposits his seed in my freshly opened chute.

When he collapses on my back, I have to ask him to move, so I can breathe. I'm amazed when he rolls over, and I see the size of his dick. I can't believe it's been inside me. It's too thick for me to get my hand around and must be at least ten inches long. I run my hand up and down the slick shaft watching the remains of his load ooze out of the meatus.

"That was some fuck, dude," he says. "You the first piece I've had since I've been inside. I'm still fucking horny – but let's take a shower first."

I pick up the lube and head upstairs. He pushes me down on the treads, grabs my nuts and cock between my legs, and then glues his mouth to my asshole. He growls like a dog as he chews on my tender hole. I bend over as far as possible and push my rear-end into his face. I hope he's going to fuck me again.

His face is covered with ass-juice when he releases me and pulls me to my feet. When we enter the shower, we are both hard. He pulls me into his arms and French kisses me as the water cascades over our aroused bodies.

Later, in the bedroom, we fall into one another's arms. He swivels around into a sixty-nine position, rolling on top of me with his knees on either side of my head.

As he deep-throats me, I run my tongue around the shiny head of his rod, and slurp up his precum. I pull the big knob into my mouth, and try to deep throat him. His beautiful hairy cleft, spread before my eyes, beckons me, so I pull his asshole to my mouth, nibble on the smooth fissure and run my tongue into his dilated hole.

"Fuck, that feels good," he groans. "I wan' you inside me again."

He lubricates my shaft, moves onto his back, and pulls his legs up to his chest, so I can fuck him. Quicker than a wink, I'm balls deep in his silky chute, fucking him as though he's my last piece of tail. He hooks his legs behind his elbows and strokes his shaft in time to my deep pistoning. His cock-head is close to my mouth, so I bend over and suck him as I fuck his ass.

"Don't come," he says. "I wanna fuck you again."

My cock slips out of his chute when he lowers his legs.

"Sit on me," he says, smearing lube over his big boner.

I straddle his body, lower myself onto his upright pole, and then lean back on my hands and ride him like a cowboy on a wild mustang. His cock's stimulating something deep inside me that I've never felt before. My hard rod, leaking precum, bounces up and down. There's a surprised look on his face when cum suddenly erupts from my dick and splatters his face and neck. I can't believe it myself. Except for wet dreams, I've never come without touching my dick.

He rams me hard and fast for a moment, and then cries out, "I'm coming. I'm coming."

Exhausted, I fall on top of him. Jerking-off was never this much fun. When I roll off his body, I can feel his hot cum trickling from my ravished chute.

I glance over at the clock and am astonished to see we have been on the go for a couple of hours. He has to be back for roll call, so he quickly dresses and leaves. After he's gone, I realize I don't know his name or the reason for his incarceration.

Over the next few days, I'm thinking about him constantly, and all my jerk-off sessions are a reliving of the time we spent together. If I don't see him again I'll go crazy. I devise a plan to get him back. When my father is out of the house, I go downstairs and sabotage the air-conditioner.

When my father returns, he says. "Don't tell me the damn thing is broken again?"

"Maybe we should get that inmate back?" I say.

"Can't do that," he says.

I hope nothing has happened to him.

"Why not?"

"He's being released this afternoon. It turns out the only thing he is guilty of, was being in the wrong place, at the wrong time. The police arrested a man yesterday. He has confessed that it was he, not Craig Jones, who committed the robbery."

That afternoon I'm in my father's car, outside the main gates of the prison, waiting for Craig.

When he comes out, I drive over to him and swing the passenger door open. "You need a ride handsome?" I ask.

He's glowing when he jumps into the car, and squeezes my thigh. "I was hoping to see you again, but I wasn't sure whether you'd want to see me."

"Try keeping me away," I say.

BUTT IN
By Landon Dixon

I waded to the top of the sand dune, looked down, and there he was – laid out on the beach like a Nubian offering to the glute gods. He was all by himself, sheltered by a set of dunes, flat on his stomach on a white towel, his ebony body shining under the hot sun, his thong-split butt cheeks gleaming like twin licorice orbs.

I went weak in the knees, hard in the cock.

I'm an assman from way back. Men's rears have always held a fearsome attraction for me. I've gravitated to their moons for as long as I can remember, following them with my eyes in pants and shorts and swimsuits, fondling them with my hands, clothed and bare, fucking them with my cock. While some men are beachcombers, scouring the shimmering sands for lost treasure, I'm a buttcomber, the beach just one of the many places where I pursue my passion for male posterior. And here I'd hit the jackpot.

This man's served-up ass was one of the most luscious I'd ever seen, the thin red line of his thong accentuating the massiveness and moundedness of his humps, cleaving them depthlessly down the middle and swelling them up into stunning relief.

I waded down the crumbling side of the dune on crumbling legs, closer to the man with the burnished thunder cheeks; moving silently, stealthily, his buttocks looming ever larger in my widened eyes. It was mid-morning, beachgoers on either side of the sand dunes, laughing and splashing and chasing each other around. But as I drew nearer to the man and his cheeks, the sound of blood pounding in my heads, my heart in my chest, blocked out the rolling surf and public noise.

Although I did hear one other thing – the light snoring of the butt-blessed dude stretched out facedown on the towel. He was sleeping!

I could barely contain my excitement, the huge bulge in the front of my knee-length swim trunks. I'd thought I'd have to go waist-deep in the ocean to fully take advantage of this precious sighting; jack into the surf as I stared at the double-hilled shoreline. But now a bolder plan took hold in my dirty mind, like my hand on my cock rubbing through my swimsuit. I approached the dozing man from the rear.

I stood right in between his splayed legs on his towel, gazing down at him, at his huge buttocks rising up to meet me. He had a shaved head, a gold earring in his right ear, his torso and legs long and lean and coal-black. His face rested on his folded hands, his eyes closed and mouth slightly open.

Now, I'm not a bad-looking guy myself – tall and thin, with brown hair and blue eyes, an attractive if tense face, a large, easily-aroused cock. So I could have sat down on the sand next to the guy and introduced myself and maybe gotten to know him, gone up the beach for a coke and a hot dog. Only, that would've taken time and a set of social skills, and I'm short on both. Besides, men are asses to me (in the finest sense of the word), nothing more, nothing less. Relationships are for other guys not always hot on the trail for tail.

So, impulsively, needfully and uncontrollably, I pushed my swimsuit down to my ankles and hefted my heavy, hanging cock, started stroking. Right out there in the open on the beach, under the spell of those glorious globes.

The guy went right on gently snoring, as I glared at his overstuffed seat cushions and pumped my hand up and down the pulsating length of my dong. The sun was to the side of us, so my shadows didn't cross him and them, reveal my presence. I yearned to touch the heaped-up flesh, ply it, fill my sweating hands with glistening cheek and rub and squeeze and knead; and then fill my mouth, kissing and licking and biting; and then my dick, frotting and fucking. But I didn't dare. Even I, butt appraiser and appreciator of the universe, had that much restraint, at least. The dude looked tough.

I cupped a smooth, tingling pec, rolled a buzzing, tan nipple, my body inflamed with more heat than even the sun could generate, caressing my cock in slow, sensuous strokes from shaven balls up to mushroomed hood. I was poled out full-length now, a length almost as impressive as the height and depth and width of the man's butt cheeks. He was completely oblivious to me jacking over top of him. I dropped down onto my knees, in between his legs, closer to his ass.

The rounded peaks of his shining buttocks were only a mere, mouthwatering foot or so from the end of my jacked-up cock. I trembled all over despite the inferno heat, pumping faster, harder, fisting my rod. I gripped my balls and squeezed, twisted. But that was no good, because it raised my dick, that one inch taking me farther away from the lush, dark mounds of my desire. So I pinched a nipple, pulled on it, tugging cock with relentless abandon.

My balls tightened and tingled. Sweat poured down my face and the sides of my body, damp palm flying along my cum-hard prick, my heavy breathing and the 'thwack-thwack' of flesh on flesh now filling the supercharged air.

Then I jerked, and jetted, my over-stimulated prick going off in my hand.

For a split-second rationale thought entered my addled mind and told me to spray away from the sprawled-out dude. But my balls and cock and warped soul were having none of it. I bit my lip to bleeding and rained white-hot cum down on the man's ass, splashing his magnificent buttocks, striping the dark meat with white, burning his taut, towering skin with my lust. Jolted again and again, I coated his ass with sticky adulation.

His eyes popped open, and he shook his head. He rose up on his elbows and turned and groggily looked at me. I did the only thing I could do, which is what I'd wanted to do all along – I plunged my hands down onto his buttocks and started rubbing. "Looked like you could use some more suntan lotion!" I gulped, rubbing my heated semen into the guy's ass.

He swallowed and blinked his big brown eyes at me, the muscles on his shoulders and back rippling, his butt cheeks tightening deliciously under my hands. "Yeah, uh, thanks, man," he said in a rich, deep timbre. "But that doesn't really explain why your dong's hanging out."

I looked down. My cock was still stretched out in the open, swaying with the rhythm of kneading hands. I'd forgotten to tuck myself back in. "Uh ..."

He grinned, teeth gleaming, feasting his eyes on my meat. "You like a built booty, huh? I like a big dick, myself. Name's Doug."

"B-Brent," I stammered.

Doug rolled over onto his back and gestured at me and my cock. I frowned. His ass was gone from view, out of my hands. But I had to honor the man's request, after he'd given me so much pleasure. I straddled his body and crawled up his chest until my cock dangled directly over his mouth, hood brushing his lips.

He blew on my cap, and I jerked. He reached his hand around and laced his long fingers around my shaft, and I jumped. He started gliding his warm, smooth palm up and down my prick.

"Yes!" I breathed.

"Yeah," he murmured, my cock swelling harder, pulsing in his stroking hand. Recovery time is never an issue with me when I'm in the presence of gluteness.

Out of the corner of my eye, I spotted a pair of teenaged boys crest the dune to my right, just as Doug brought his head up and pulled mine down, slid his thick lips over my bloated knob. I groaned, the boys holding their beach ball between them and staring at us. I didn't mind their watching, I welcomed it, overwhelmed by the hot, wet sensation of Doug's mouth on my cock. I arched my back and threw my arms up into the air in exultation, thrusting my hips forward, sinking my dong deep into Doug's mouth.

If I have a limitless capacity for ass worship – which I do – this guy had an almost limitless capacity for cock. He swallowed me down to the base, my balls coming to rest on his chin. His liquid eyes shone up at me, plush lips sealed tight, my pole locked down in the heated, velvety confines of his mouth and throat. Then he started moving his head, and mouth, sucking on my prick.

Doug wet-vacced me in long, deep pulls. My shaft glistened with his saliva, the throbbing meat oiling in and out of him, his lips tugging, tongue cushioning, mouth enveloping and eating. I gripped my own clenched butt cheeks and pumped, fucking his face as he sucked on my cock.

The boys nervously laughed and ran off. I almost hoped they'd bring their parents and some paying customers back with them to watch. I wanted everyone to see what I was feeling. It was too good to be stopped – Doug's sucking meeting my pumping in an erotic crescendo, the sweet music of man-lust being played on my cock.

After taking me down his throat and hard-sucking me to the very edge of orgasm, Doug suddenly pulled my dick right out of his molten mouth. I strained slick and beating in his hand, his noosing fingers at the base of my cock bottling my juices. He smiled up at me, tonguing a pearl drop of precum from my yawning slit and smacking his lips and swallowing; then swirling his neon-pink sticker around and around my cockhead, making the both of us dizzy.

"I bet you'd like to drive this slab up my ass, huh, Brent?" he growled, reading my blown mind.

His throaty voice reverberated all along my cock and all through my body. I bobbed my head up and down like a buttman in a communal shower.

Doug blossomed his lips over my knob again and tugged a couple more times. Before gesturing at me to get up and off. When I did, he rolled back over onto his front and arched his bum up like a bitch in heat.

I was his butt-bitch, and I was in heat!

I straddled his legs and grabbed onto his ass. "Yes!" I yelped, clutching the thick, hot, heavy flesh. I let the smooth, stretched skin melt into my hands. Then I started massaging, rubbing the padded masses, my cock an iron staff in between my legs and over his.

He groaned into his hands, as I caressed, kneaded, groped, sunk my fingers into his butt meat, poured my palms all over. His cheeks were still slick with my semen, and I used that to my advantage, sliding my hands up and down his bloated pillows.

Then I grabbed them tight where they first swelled up from the backs of his legs and squeezed them upwards and upwards, the gleaming flesh gliding, towering in my hands. Until I popped off at their breathtaking highest elevations, and they shuddered back down into hillock formation.

I lightly spanked one cheek, the other, just to watch them gyrate. Then I bent my head down and bit into the right one, the left, filling my drooling mouth with the ripe, heated flesh. Doug jerked, trembling like his cheeks, and I shot out my tongue and licked all over the taut, twin surfaces, tasting my sperm and his skin. I plucked his thong out of his crack with my teeth and shot the gap with my tongue, plunging it wet and wild into his bum cleavage, washing up and down his smooth crack.

"Fuck!" he grunted.

"Not yet," I breathed, getting a real good taste of the man, the best way I knew how.

Gripping his cheeks with my greasy fingers, I spread them apart. His anus split open before me, deep and dark and yummy. I plugged my tongue in, corkscrewing into his pucker. His butt jumped up, my tongue plowing deeper. I squirmed it around inside the man, rimming his inner walls with an ardor and aptitude he'd probably never experienced before.

"Fuck!" he rasped. "And I mean it!" He was pumping the towel and sand with his cock, grinding away as I ate out his ass.

I withdrew and applied my tongue to his crack again, lapping from deep in between his legs to the top of his tailbone, getting a few more good licks in. Before slathering his crack and my cock with tanning oil, gearing and greasing ourselves up for the next phase.

I finally released his butt and draped my body over top of his. I would've preferred doggy-style, to see his bum shimmying with delight as I banged it, but he was punishing his towel with a furious intensity. So I gripped my slickened dick and split his pumping cheeks with my hood. He reached back and spread 'em, and I pressed into his manhole, holding my breath. Then I burst through his ring and into his anus, making both of us groan.

I sank the entire length and width of my dong into his chute, slowly, surely, stunningly. The heat was incredible, the tightness immense. I bulged his swollen ass with my cock and joyously rutted around back there for a moment before digging my hands into the towel on either side of him and pumping my hips, fucking his butt.

The sun beat down on us, the air crackling with the smack of my clenched thighs against his bountiful buttocks, as I drove my dong back and forth in his anus. I sawed slow and sensual, letting his ass suck on my prick, kissing his cheeks with my body. Then I pistoned hard and fast, bouncing off his behind, ruthlessly reaming him. He pumped the ground in rhythm to me plundering his rump, never missing a frenzied beat.

I vibrated with exertion and feeling, pounding my cock into the man's gripping, superheated chute until I furiously pumped right past the point of no return. "I'm coming, Doug!" I bleated.

"Come in my ass!" he roared, thundering into the sand.

I shot at last, loving look down at my body spanking off his beautiful mounds, my cock diving into his hole. And then I cried, "Yes!" jerking, jolted by wicked orgasm, exploding in the man's ass.

I blazed liquid fire into Doug's anus, filling him 'til I was wallowing in my own juices. He shuddered and shook with his own orgasm, spraying into his thong and towel, staining the sand, the pair of us blowing out our balls out there on the beach.

"Hey, you're not going to stay for awhile?" he asked with surprise afterwards. He was rolled over onto his side, his butt partially hidden.

I was already on my feet, my trunks pulled back up. "Uh, sorry, but I've got to get going."

There were too many men, two plump cheeks on each, and too little time.

READY FOR PLAY
By R. W. Clinger

1. CREAMING THE KLEINS

I bump into Sampson Young of McCardle and Young Architecture as he exits the elevator on the seventh floor. Mr. Young drops the files in his hands and shares some severe eye contact with me that says he can fire me for running into him. Both of us hunch down to pick up the files and almost brush our foreheads together. I collect a few of the files, and he collects the rest. Now, we stand face-to-face, assistant paper pushing boy and co-owner in an eye draw.

Helplessly, I take in his almond-colored eyes, bushy eyebrows, wide nose, and adorable red lips. My eyes scan his six-two frame and 200 pounds of muscle from his three workouts a week. I calculate the width of his hairless chest at forty inches with erect nipples and cut abs. The lead architect is thirty-three years old, new at running his firm, and … is totally irresistible with his coconut brown skin and pearly white grin.

"I'm clumsy, Mr. Young. My apologies." I pass the files to my boss.

"I rather like clumsy guys," he says and catches me off guard. "Being clumsy makes us all comprehend that we're real. No fakes. No uppity airs. Bottom line: we are all equal."

He checks me out from head to toe: five-eleven Jamaican frame, twenty-three years old, amethyst-blue eyes shaped like olives, walnut-colored skin, fresh buzz cut, medium-size build, 170 pounds, tie askew, a morning coffee stain near my left nipple from another clumsy act. He licks his lips while he holds his files, winks at me, smiles, and asks, "You went to Temple, right?"

I did and consider it the best school in Philly. Four years of fun in my life. "You also went to Temple, didn't you, Mr. Young?"

He tells me he graduated in 2003 with a degree in architecture and asks if I like to build things.

I do; I concentrate on gay bed and breakfasts ... and erections on steamy dark-skinned men.

"What happened to your shirt?" He moves up to me and touches the coffee stain with two fingers; it's total sexual harassment to the nth degree, but what the fuck do I care since he's Mr. Gorgeous.

"A coffee spill while going through my e-mail this morning."

"I can take care of this," he confirms, pulls a shirttail out of my navy slacks, and gently caresses two of my abs.

I grow hard almost immediately, since I've prohibited myself from men for the last six months because Xaviar Bond broke my heart. "How do you intend to take care of it, Mr. Young?"

He tells me to follow him into his office, which I do. The dapper man closes the door behind us and locks it; action that doesn't normally happen in the corporate world between a boss and his employee for fear of a lawsuit. "Mr. Young, I really think ..." I begin to challenge him.

But he immediately spins around, grazes his chest against my chest, almost touches my forehead with his plump lips, stares down at me, and informs, "This is a private meeting, Cam. No one on our team needs to know what happens between two adult men behind a closed door."

"Mr. Young, are you hitting on me?" I sound naïve and simple-minded but sexy at the same time. In fact, I sound like a little boy who is still wet behind the ears and has never been kissed.

"Cam Fielding, do you want a position as a partner with this firm in the future?" He starts to unbutton my coffee-stained shirt, making sure his fingertips graze my sculpted chest.

It's a ridiculous question, since he knows I do. "Are you blackmailing me, sir?"

"You can say that. Some men who have passed through this firm have received the highest recommendations from me." He pulls my shirt and T-shirt over my shoulders and drops both to the Berber carpet; clearly he has no intention of eradicating its coffee stain.

Before I can object, the firm's partner finds one of my light cocoa-colored nipples and offers it a squeeze. A gasp suddenly exits my mouth, and he inquires, "You like that, don't you?"

"I do, sir."

His free hand finds my other nipple, and he provides it with a gentle twist. In doing so, he inquires, "You're shivering. Do I make you nervous?"

"You do, sir."

He lightly chuckles, strums both the quarter-sized nipples, and keeps them firm. This time he asks, "Do I make you hard?" and his right hand falls down and over my cut chest, against the tiny stubs of freshly shaved treasure trail hair, over my Kenneth Cole belt buckle, and eventually lands on the erect goods between my legs. He rolls a palm around the swollen extension of slacks-covered cock and chants, "My God, I do make you hard."

What he doesn't know – I shoot three bubbles of pre-spew into my cotton briefs, excited by his handy work. And, I want to kiss his handsome face, connect my assistant lips with his partner ones, and seal us together with a common queer bond.

We don't kiss, though. Instead, I continue to shiver, and he decides to unbutton the belt buckle that secures my slacks up. His hands work fast and in a diligent manner. Before I know it, the buckle is loose and ... he unbuttons my J.Crew slacks and unzips their golden zipper. What he finds beneath is no surprise: nine inches of hard pole tucked inside Calvin Klein basic briefs.

"Nice," the executive whispers while he massages the cotton-covered dog inside his palm.

"This is totally against company policy, Mr. Young," I whimper and feel more bubbles of ooze leak out of my hose.

"When you own half the company, Mr. Fielding, there are no policies."

Unbeknownst to me, my J.Crews are pulled down to my ankles, and the architect falls to his knees. Being cordial, he leans his face against my firm rod, opens his mouth, and rolls his lips over the cotton's fabric.

I gasp for breath above him, and waver to and fro. Windblown, at a loss for words, I almost lose my balance and topple to the Berber. My fingers find his shoulders to stay upright in front of him. Dizzy and confused, I heave for oxygen. More bubbles of pre-leak jet out of my rod.

The Temple graduate moans and groans beneath me. His right hand finds my brief-covered balls and provides the duo with some light massaging. His other hand rolls up and along my chest, meets my navel, abs, and now my left nipple, which he kindly squeezes.

Catching my breath, I find the strength to mutter, "If you don't stop … if you don't pull off of me, Mr. Young … I'm going to come."

The professional architect pulls away from me and murmurs, "Go for it. Shoot your load," and cheers me on.

As more mouth motion ensues on my material-hidden shaft, I thrust my hips against his face and bang my briefs off his skin. One … two … three shifts occur, an airy gasp, and … a final grunt escapes my mouth as I fill my cotton with man-sap, creaming the Kleins.

"A job well done," he praises after he pulls away from my goods and smiles up at my spent face.

I do believe our private encounter is over but discover that I'm very wrong. Still positioned on his knees, the firm's partner says, "Let me help you out," and pulls the rim down on my briefs. He exposes a cream factory beneath: rod and balls and V-patch of black curly pubic hair against my Jamaican skin are covered in white juice. The sticky substance clings to my veined cock and its mushroom-shaped head.

Again, Mr. Young whispers, "Nice." After this single compliment, he finally stands, reaches forward with his right hand, wraps his palm and fingers around my beef, begins to use slow strokes on the tool, and massages my spent into its skin, and his fingers. In doing so, he admits, "You're a hot little fucker. I don't know how I'm going to be able to keep my hands off you."

"I'm a mess," I whisper, gasp for air, and enjoy his slow handjob.

"You take the rest of the day off with pay. I'll see that your work gets done. How does that sound?"

"Like nepotism."

He chuckles, pulls his gunk-covered palm and fingers away from my tool, and admits, "Sometimes you have to take what's given to you … no matter what it is."

"Trust me, I'm not complaining," I reply, pull up my briefs and slacks, zip and button up, happy to have the rest of the day off and gain a position of being Mr. Young's pet in the process.

2. PENIS PET

For the next two weeks, Mr. Young watches me. Not what my multitasking entails. Not what I produce at the end of my workdays. Not how I apply myself at his firm. Instead, the guy studies my chest, legs, arms, pretty boy Jamaican face, and whatnot. He follows me to the lunch room to buy a Diet Pepsi, to the copy room to fetch a few supplies, and down to Ray's Gym for a workout after my eight hours at the firm.

A rumor spreads around the office by other assistants that I'm his penis pet.

"Cam is sucking and fucking his way up the corporate ladder with his black ass good looks."

"You know Young is doing push-ups on that boy."

"Every time Cam sucks Mr. Young's cock, he's making more in his paycheck."

Fuck the rumors. Who cares? I don't. And, I believe Mr. Young doesn't care either.

Two weeks after my office-gig with Mr. Young, he follows me into the men's room and locks the door behind us. I stand at the urinal with my goods out and take a mid-morning piss. The door's click startles me, and I realize the executive's sexual acts are about to continue. He cuddles his cock against my ass and places his chin on my Ralph Lauren polo-covered shoulder. His right hand reaches around my middle. and he grabs onto my wanker. He says, "I'm the make-sure-you-shake-it police. How's everything going on in here?"

Honestly, I'm done with my piss and shake my hose. I turn my head slightly to the right and my face meets his face. I take in his strong and sexy cologne and whisper, "Mr. Young, I thought you were the rump police?"

Ready for play, he grabs my ass with his left palm and provides my bulbous bottom with a firm squeeze. "I take on as many positions as I can."

"The go-getter in this company, I guess it's why you're in charge."

My neck is gently kissed and now licked. Mr. Young whispers, "Mmmmmm ... You're quite tasty."

"I'm a buffet for you, aren't I?"

"What can I say? I have an irresistible weakness for chocolate office boys."

I begin to stuff my goods back into my Aussiebum briefs and slacks, but the architect has other things on his mind. He gently pulls my slacks down to my ankles with my cotton briefs and ...

"Mr. Young, what's happening back there?" I feel his slender nose and somewhat big lips against my showered rump and know that he smells some Lever 2000 on my skin. His tongue protrudes from his mouth and laps at both of my cheeks in a feisty manner, which causes me to feel a bit dizzy.

"I'm studying your blueprints, Cam. Why don't you help me out and spread your legs a little."

I oblige. Why not? Maybe I can land a partner position in years to come if I keep this sexual affair with the hot executive going. It's worth the try, right? Happily, I spread my legs as he instructs: "Bend over and place your palms on the tile wall, Mr. Fielding."

I listen; always such a good employee. He spreads my ass cheeks with his fingers and rolls his tongue around my man-hole. Heavy slurps develop behind me. He licks and laps at its surface in the most productive manner, and obeys his thirst. Seven swirls of his tongue turn into two dozen.

"Jesus," I moan in front of him, numb by his tongue tour. "Your team calls me your penis pet. Did you know that?"

He comes off my ass for air and admits, "I was the one who started that rumor. I'm glad it's circulating well."

I lightly laugh because of his confession, but the chuckle dissipates quite quickly as his tongue enters my behind and causes me pure elation. One thrust with his sliver of protruding tongue rotates in my rump, followed by another and another. I gasp and groan in front of him, wiggle my bottom, and murmur, "Deeper ... Push it in deeper."

And, so this is done. He bolts his face into my rump, pulls away, and continues this action for the next five … seven … eleven minutes, and pivots me into an irreversible position of man-pleasure.

After this mouth-to-ass suction, he backs away from me and says, "I dig you, penis pet."

I kindly giggle in front of him, keep my palms firm against the tile, and add, "Damn, you've built a tower between my legs."

"Be an achiever and turn around, Cam. Let me see what you're bringing to the table today for discussion." He grasps my hips, spins me around with some tender force, and inspects my upright goods that equal nine hard inches of corporate fun. "Nice work," he whispers, falls under my rod's spell, and into the meat between my legs.

"What do you plan on doing with it, Mr. Young?"

"It depends if you want a raise or not." He pulls my pick down, releases it, and it flings up and snaps against my torso. In doing so, a bubble of pre-juice flies out of its mushroom-shaped cap and twirls over my boss's head.

"A raise is never out of the question, of course."

"It's good to know you have goals, Mr. Fielding," he chants, toys with my balls in his right hand, and enjoys this restroom affair with me.

"What's on your agenda, sir?" I ask, cutting to the chase. "Do you want me to fuck you or what?"

"Going for the gusto, aren't you?" he looks up at me with his model-perfect eyes and inquires, smiling from ear to ear with a hint of hunger in his tone.

"It's a dog eat dog world in this business, and there's no reason to by shy." I honestly don't know where this comment comes from, but then again, I don't usually stand in the men's room and sport a firm wanker between my legs for my boss to stroke, lick, or suck.

"As my pet, I think it's time to feed and water you," he shares. He stands, places his lips against mine, melts me with a kiss, pulls away, and instructs, "Get on your knees and eat me."

A raise looks pretty solid in my future if I carry out this simple sex act in the restroom. Or, I can be fired if I don't oblige. Unemployment from McCardle and Young Architecture is not out of his equation. I want to keep my job and have the opportunity to gain a raise. Why would I not blow the boss, especially since I find him sexy-hot and right for my needs?

He pushes me to my knees, unzips his goods, and presents his ten inches of uncut and cocoa-colored shaft for my pleasure. The architect instructs, "Open your mouth, and let me fuck you, Mr. Fielding."

I honestly don't have the opportunity to object because the partner of the firm bolts his ten inches into my mouth and presses it down the back of my throat with exceptional force.

Mr. Young humps his junk into my face, pulls out, and humps it into my hole again. The tube of protein slides down the back of my throat and builds friction. Above me, he hangs onto my shoulders, gasps for air, and becomes overexcited by our bathroom bond. He utters between clenched teeth, "Eat me, Cam … Do it."

We work together to and fro, and build up a fine rhythm between us. East and west motion develops, which is energetic and mouth- and mind-numbing. We mix in a wild manner: suck and fuck; saliva drips to the floor; fingertips lock on shoulders; so naughty together, as one.

Perspiration gathers on his black torso as his heaves and moans intensify. Mr. Young blasts my face again and again and wills himself to meet his orgasm.

I gag and grunt as the architect slides his ten inches of beef down the back of my throat. Numbness takes over my lips, mouth, and cheeks. Satisfied with my work, I clamp my palms on the man's hips and let him ride my face until …

"Exploding," he warns, and quickly pulls out of my mouth. He aims his dog's head at my right cheek, jacks his rod a few times, and explains, "It's time for a facial."

Gasping for air, I confess, "You're a hard worker, sir. I'm ready for your shoot."

After a few hand-jacks, he blows. His spray decorates the side of my face. Cream dribbles down and over my cheek and neck, and misses my mouth by just a few millimeters. Hungry for his own spunk, he leans over, holds my chin with his right palm, extends his crimson-red tongue, and has a mid-morning snack of bittersweet ooze.

Beneath him, I say, "Something tells me you've done this before."

He swallows down some of his seed and responds, "How do you think I got through Temple?"

I stand from our connection, ready for clean-up, laugh, and add, "A man's got to do what a man's got to do at this place, Mr. Young. I understand your play."

3. DESK DUTY

Two days later, I sit in Mr. Young's office across from him and share a get-together on the topic of an uppity spa the firm is currently designing for one of our clients. Once he shares our goals with me regarding the spa, I prattle, "You're using me, and I want a little more out of the deal."

"Using you?" he questions, raises an eyebrow, and shares a handsome smile.

"You're using my cock for your satisfaction, and I want a little more out of it."

He reclines in his leather chair and chortles, "You're kidding me, right?"

"Do I sound like I'm kidding you?"

"Are you blackmailing me, Mr. Fielding?"

A greedy smile now forms on my face. I place my note taking instruments aside, loosen my tie, unbutton my Traveler pinpoint button down shirt and expose some of my chocolate-colored skin, which includes one nipple, a few abs, and my dented navel. "Of course I am not blackmailing you, sir. A man in my underling position would never demonstrate such an act." I unbuckle my leather belt, peal my slacks open, reach into my cotton briefs, and pull out a half-swollen fig-brown piece of timber, which is ready for some hardcore play.

"And, now you're attempting to seduce me?"

"What can I say?" I shrug a shoulder, and continue to control our appointment. "I know how to get by in the corporate world." I stroke my post up and down, horny as hell. A bubble of pre-sap leaks out of its smooth head, which I collect on my left index finger and lick away.

"Obviously, you now have my balls in a sling, don't you? What do you want from me?" He stands and sports a boner in his Brooks Brothers slacks the size of the Eastman Building, a McCardle and Young project that just ended this past spring.

"Another week of vacation and a twenty percent raise added to my salary."

"You cut a hard bargain, kid. Do you know that?"

I nod my head and say, "I know that you want me to carry out some desk duty." I now stand, sport my nine inches of fun, supply it with a stroke … two strokes … three strokes … and ask in a professional manner, "Mr. Young, will you be fucking me over your desk today?"

"I do believe I will, Mr. Fielding."

I walk around his desk, leash a palm over his slacks-covered rod, give his crank a firm squeeze, look my boss in his dreamy eyes, and insist, "Bang me hard, or don't do it at all, sir. My time is valuable."

In a matter of seconds, my shirt is ripped from my torso and tossed to the floor. Crumpled cotton lies in a ball on his Berber carpet. His lips meet my neck in a vampiric manner. The lips now connect with one nipple, the second nipple, eventually fall away, and he rattles off, "This is why I hired you."

"I thought it was to build things together."

He tightly cups his inflated goods, bounces the slacks-covered meat in his palm, and admits, "Trust me, we are building things together."

"But, sir, I thought …"

My comment is cut off with such hungry zeal for my flesh as he turns me around and positions me over his desk. Nipples and abs meet the walnut finish over the plane of wood where he works his sixty-plus hours a week. My bottom is grasped with his two palms and gently spanked a number of times. I'm called his penis pet and other naughty names, loving every minute of this meeting with him.

Behind me, the architect undoes his slacks, drops them and his underwear to his ankles, and applies plastic protection to his man-toy.

"Fuck me," I whimper and beg for his rod to enter my hub. "And don't be nice about it."

I swear on my office bitch career that he rushes all of his ten inches into my behind with one vibrant movement. Pain shifts within my middle as lust is found. I gasp on the desk from his immediate push, catch my breath, and attempt to relax, willed to enjoy his ride.

The designer jerks to and fro, builds up a tempo, grips my hips, and rolls in and out of my center with speedy motion. Sweat flies off his chin and chest and lands against the plane of my back. He spanks me again and again and again, and calls me the nastiest names: copy-boy-whore, dick-tease-pleaser, office-cock-eater. His banging is consistent and unstoppable. His movement is wild and quixotic as he plunges himself into me, releases his tool from my core, and plunges inside yet again.

I find my own nine inches of tool between my legs and meticulously roll fingers up and down on its excess skin.

"Jack yourself off," the man calls down to me while he still rides my rear.

I'm an obedient worker, under his care between nine and five, into our office gig, and willed to do what he tells me.

Fingers move steadily on my erect flag as a glob of pre-cream spits out of my hose and decorates the carpet between my legs. Rapidly, I continue to crank my bolt with hyper motion and enjoy my own cock-gig.

The firm's partner bucks into me and presses his pubic triangle of bristly-black hairs against my bottom. He becomes wicked with his movement behind me, drives his fingernails into my sides, and humps me with a steadfast hunger that seems limitless and almost unruly.

"Do I get that extra week of vacation and salary increase?" Now the time is right to obtain a concrete answer from him, while he pounds me, of course.

"You're in, Cam. You drive a hard bargain," Mr. Young seals our deal as his cock seals itself inside my ass another time.

"Trust me … your drive is harder," I add, cringe from his weight as it bucks into my interior and causes me to reach bliss.

"Work for it, guy. Don't think you're going to get it for nothing," he chants behind me, and rocks his meat into me with spasmodic grace.

Appealingly, I become dizzy in front him, semi-unconscious. Famous architects circle my mind: Albert Khan, Kevin Roche, Mario Botta, Frank Lloyd Wright. And, architectural buildings cluster within my thoughts: Getty Center, Falling Water, Guggenheim Museum, Chrysler Building, Seagram Building, Rockefeller Center, The Gateway Arch, Sears Tower. With every thrust, pull, push, and release from, and into my bottom, I think of another random architect or building.

Truth is, while consistently being banged, I come before my boss does. A final vibration weaves through my center, spine, and between my legs. Office-sap promptly spirals out of my cock and decorates the area under his walnut desk. The shoot is endless, and a vat of my cream puddles on his floor as my man-joint empties, completely.

Because my cum-fest is too much for the architect to handle, an aphrodisiac for his sexual needs, he blasts into my rump a final time and clarifies behind me, "Firing my load."

"Shoot it," I groan, and enjoy my ride on his stick.

The man releases his junk from my hole, rips the plastic condom off his pick, tosses it to the floor, and begins to jack himself off with one … two … three strokes.

Hot spew flies against my back and sizzles on my skin. Mr. Young uses one of his hands and rubs the sticky ooze into my russet flesh, slaps my tight office bottom, and pulls me up and off the desk. He meets his mouth with my mouth and shares a mind-blowing kiss with me. Once the kiss ends, he pushes me away, and says, "Go home and clean yourself up. Come back around six, and I'll take you to dinner."

"Don't forget that I like to dance," I admit, heave for breath, and devise the rules again.

"I'm sure you like to do many things," he adds, while applying his right hand to my fig-colored cock, provides it with a little squeeze, and secretly becomes my office boyfriend for the next few years, or longer … until I land partner.

DICK
By Landon Dixon

Detective Taylor shoved the convenience store door open, walked inside. He was first on the scene. He saw the young black man with the gun pointed at his head and snorted.

"Good collar ... Matt," he said, squinting at the clerk's nametag. "You can put the heater down. I got it from here."

Matt, a tall, lanky kid of sixteen, sporting a blond thatch of hair and bright blue eyes, slowly uncocked the fully-loaded .44 Magnum with two trembling thumbs. "He thought he could rob me. But I showed him, officer."

Taylor grunted. "Store policy doesn't call for heroics, Matt. But thanks, all the same." He gripped the perp by his white T-shirt, shook him. "You got a back room, Matt? Somewhere I can view the video footage, give the rubber hose treatment to this scumbag." He grinned, shaking his captive again.

The clerk grinned back, then hustled down the hall at the rear of the store and unlocked a small office for the detective. "Here you go, officer. Need me to show you how to work the computer?"

Taylor shoved the would-be thief through the door in front of him. "Nah, I can handle it. You take care of the customers. Thanks." He looked at his prisoner, a short, muscular kid of eighteen, with black velvet skin and sullen brown eyes, a lush mouth and wide nose, close-cropped hair. "If he gets the better of me, I'll give you a holler."

Matt nodded, returned to his post behind the counter at the front of the store. The detective entered the office, closing and locking the door behind him.

"Really bungled this one, huh, Lawrence?"

The kid sat down on the edge of the small, cluttered desk inside the office, wiped his nose with the back of his hand. "How was I supposed to know Blondie out there was Dirty Harry? Like you said, store policy is let 'em have it."

Taylor ran a thick hand through his graying hair. He was forty, going on world-weary, his once rugged body trending towards paunch, the pouches under his grey eyes testimony to too much time on the job, trying to hold things together. It wasn't easy working both sides of the street, and keeping from getting caught. "You got nothing, I suppose?"

"What'd you think?"

"Going to be tough getting you out of this jam … without any payoff."

A cynical grin creased Lawrence's thick lips. Then he went down on his knees in front of Taylor, deftly tugged the detective's fly down, pulled the detective's cock out. The pink appendage was already half-swollen, getting thicker. Lawrence dipped his head down and caught the beefy cap in his mouth and sucked on it.

Taylor jerked at the wet-hot impact of the other's mouth on his sensitive appendage. But he pulled it back out, slapped Lawrence's cheek with it. "Got to give you the rubber hose treatment, remember? For being a bad boy." He slapped Lawrence's other cheek with the stiffening rod.

The kid stared up at him, easily taking the hosing, Taylor's cock briskly beating against his cheeks, brushing past his lips. The detective quickly surged to full erection, striking Lawrence's soft, smooth skin. He dragged the mushroomed head of his dick across the young man's mouth, slowing on the wet, plush lips, then dragging back the other way. Only this time, he stopped his cockhead at Lawrence's open mouth, let it beat there on his lips, basking in the warm, humid breath.

Then he pushed forward, blossoming Lawrence's lips with his knob, shoving his hood inside the kid's mouth. Lawrence sealed his lips around the bloated cap and sucked on it again.

"That's the stuff," Taylor grunted, running his big hands over the young man's head, pulling that head closer, his cock rising up in Lawrence's mouth.

The man on his knees planted his sweaty, pale palms on Taylor's thighs, bobbed his head back and forth. He took the older man's meat right down to the hairy balls, pulled back, tugging tightly, wetly on the surging dong. He'd done it many times before, so he knew exactly what Taylor liked. He sunk his teeth into the blood-engorged shaft just below the hood and made as if he was going to bite the purpled knob right off.

"Fucking right, kid!" Taylor growled, staring down at the teenager with his cockhead between his teeth. "You going to bite the dick that feeds you?" He tingled from head to toe, an aging adrenaline junkie who got his kicks anywhere he could find them now.

Lawrence wagged his head back and forth, pulling Taylor's cock with him, teeth just scratching the surface of shaft. Then he held the man's cock straight, looking up at him, and moved his head slowly forward, swallowing Taylor's prick. Vein-popped shaft glided in between his stretched lips, his mouth consuming more and more overswollen inches. Until his nose was nuzzling balls again.

Taylor watched, shaking, the depth of the delicious wet heat getting even to him. He pumped his hips, thrusting his hood down Lawrence's velvety throat, fucking the kid's face.

Lawrence's nostrils flared for air, his fingernails digging into Taylor's thighs. But he didn't back off, didn't gag, letting the man saw away at his mouth and throat with that pumped, pulsating cock.

Taylor groaned, plumbing depths of depravity he'd never imagined when he'd first joined the force as a rookie so many years ago. But the temptations had been just too many, the power too absolute. He churned Lawrence's wet-hot mouth, sliding his dick along the young man's slick, beaded tongue. Then he grabbed his cock at the base and ripped it out of the kid's mouth with a pop.

"You going to do better next time?" he rasped, slapping Lawrence's face with his glistening dong.

Lawrence grinned pure white teeth up at the sweating man, showed him the neon-pink cavern of his mouth, the length of his tongue.

Taylor unnoosed the base of his iron-hard rod, stroked. He buckled, semen spurting out of the tip of his prong and striping Lawrence's tongue, shooting into the teenager's mouth. He came hard and heavy in the kid's face, bucking against the closed door of the tiny back room.

Afterwards, Taylor escorted Lawrence out of the store and shoved him up against his undercover car to be handcuffed. But the kid jabbed a well-timed elbow into Taylor's gut, doubling the detective over. Lawrence streaked off into the night.

Taylor jammed the clerk's .44 up into the air just in time, before the guy could squeeze off a round. "Don't sweat it," he said. "I'll catch up with him. I don't let these punks get away ... for long."

# # # # #

Two convenience stores were knocked over the next week, successfully; the take small but not insignificant. Taylor waited for Lawrence at their usual rendezvous spot – a darkened doorway in an abandoned projects highrise – but Lawrence didn't show.

Taylor went on the prowl. He'd seen it before, knew where to look – alleys, parked cars, shitholes. He'd been on the force too long to let one of his 'boys' get the better of him.

He asked around, scouring the 'hoods where delinquents hung out, gangs banged. He rousted fuckpads and shooting galleries, picking up plenty of illegal drugs and guns on his crusade. It just looked like a righteous cop doing more than his level-best to track down a criminal.

Finally, he spotted illicit activity in an alley off Kershaw one lonely night, shone his car light on the sordid scene. It was Lawrence, fucking some punk up the ass, the next downlink in the food chain of survival on the streets.

Taylor gunned the undercover car and roared into the alley, sending the rats and punks scurrying. He barreled out of the vehicle and collared Lawrence by the back of his jeans, as the young man was desperately trying to tug them up, so he could run faster.

"Caught with your pants down, huh?" Taylor wheezed, watching the other teenager gazelle down the alley and out the

61

other side. He licked his chops at the sight of those taut, twitching cheeks in the short-shorts. New meat on his beat.

Taylor turned off the light and slammed Lawrence up against the alley wall. "Where's my take from the two scores?" he gritted in the young man's ear.

"I spent it," Lawrence spat back. He tried to spin around, go for Taylor's cock already tenting the front of his pants.

"Uh-huh," Taylor responded, shoving Lawrence back up against the wall. "You owe me more than that. You're going to get what's really coming to you this time."

Lawrence planted his hands up against the grimy wall and wiggled his ass. Taylor yanked the teenager's jeans all the way down, exposing dark, ripe ass mounds. He gripped them, squeezed them, sinking his fingers into the pliable masses. Lawrence groaned.

Taylor unzipped and pulled his baton out of his pants. He was hard as he'd ever been, a back alley fuck something special. He whacked Lawrence's night-shaded buttocks with his shining pink dong, watching them ripple, feeling them ripple.

"Yeah, fuck me in the ass, pig!" Lawrence hissed, just like the jaded cop liked it.

"Want me to stick your ass, huh, punk!?" he rasped in Lawrence's ear, crowding up close to the teenager. He shot his rod in between Lawrence's cheeks, jerking at the smooth, heated sensation, frotting. "Want me to fuck you in the ass, like you deserve!?"

Lawrence grunted, undulating his butt back against Taylor's shifting cock.

The detective grabbed a tube of lube out of his jacket pocket, greased his gun, glided it back into Lawrence's bum cleavage, stroking harder. Lawrence tore his hands off the brick and reached back and spread his cheeks. He shuddered as Taylor's slickened hood plugged up against his pucker.

Taylor took a quick glance around, gripping his glistening cannon at the bushy base. No one around to disturb this off-the-record interrogation. He pressed his knob up against Lawrence's bunghole, and burst through.

"Fuck!" both men moaned, mushroomed cap muscling through resisting ring.

Taylor leaned into it, shoving his shaft into Lawrence's anus, stuffing the young man with his cock. He went in hard and slow, stretching chute, bumping up against bowels.

The gripping heat made Taylor shake like Lawrence's butt cheeks. He delivered full-bore, driving his entire length into the young man's ass, pinning him to the wall, impaling him on his cock. And then he pumped, churning luscious pink sleeve.

"Fuck! Fuck!" Lawrence cried, pounding the alley wall with his clenched fists, anus getting pounded.

Sweat poured off Taylor's brow and ran down his face, his cock consumed by that hot, hungry ass, gliding back and forth in it. He gritted his teeth and moved his hips, fucking faster, harder, his body temperature soaring into the danger zone for a man with his blood pressure problems.

He drove harder still, gripping Lawrence's hips and slamming up against him over and over. His thighs smacked the young man's cheeks to shuddering, his ramming cock reaming Lawrence's chute, relentlessly, recklessly.

Lawrence was rocked back and forth by the force of the detective's sawing cock in his ass. He moaned, bouncing back, moving his ass in perfect rhythm to Taylor's thrusting, adding to the wicked onslaught.

Taylor didn't have the strength and stamina he'd had as a young cop on the beat. He belted the kid's butt a few more times, then ripped his cock free, squeezing it tight at the base. Lawrence spun around and assumed the position – on his knees, mouth open. Taylor jammed his throbbing dong into the teenager's mouth and let loose.

"Fuck, yeah!" he howled, bucking, blasting into the steaming maw.

White-hot sperm shot out of the tip of the ruptured cock and rocketed down Lawrence's throat. Taylor jerked, jolted repeatedly by the savage intensity of his orgasm, Lawrence gripping the man's hips, throat working, swallowing all evidence of the depravity.

# # # # #

Taylor shoved the kid up against the side of his vehicle and slapped the handcuffs on him.

"Hey, what the fuck you doing?" Lawrence protested, all the way to the stationhouse.

Taylor looked back at him and grinned. "You shouldn't have tried to screw me over, kid. That's my job."

At the stationhouse, the detective paraded his prisoner in front of his fellow officers. "I think we can close the books on that recent string of convenience store robberies," he said.

Lawrence stared at Taylor, ashen-faced. Then he shot off his mouth, yelling for all to hear, "This cop's dirty. He got a cut of everything I stole! He fucked me in the ass and mouth, too – whole bunch of times!"

Chief of Detectives Morgan laughed, throwing an arm around Taylor's well-rounded shoulders. "How many kids you got at home now, Jim?" he asked.

"Five already and another on the way, Chief," Taylor responded, grinning, thinking of his wife, Trudy. She'd been one of his 'girls' when he'd first started out on the beat. Until he'd taken care of her.

TAKING IT FOR THE TEAM
By Logan Zachary

"You bet your black ass?" Coach Ryan said.

My face burned as I avoided eye contact. "I know. It was a stupid bet. What can I say?"

"Nathan, a fight breaks out at the end of the basketball game that we won, and you and Sam Jenkins are yelling insults at each other, and at the height of your maturity, you bet each others' ass to the winning team? Did I get that straight?"

"It *is* the gay league…" I started, but Coach's look stopped me.

"You need to fix this, and fix this NOW! I don't want this week's Lavender to have an article about our league and your bet. Do you get me?" His finger poked into my chest.

I got him.

I met with Sam at The Eagle, hoping we could discuss this bet and call an end to it once and for all.

"Sam, Coach Ryan is pissed at me over this bet, and after thinking about it, I couldn't let our whole team use you. So I'm calling off your commitment."

Sam smiled at me. "That is so nice of you to save my ass."

I waited. Nothing else came.

Sam took a long sip on his beer. He looked around the bar. It was early, and the crowd hadn't filtered in yet.

"Sam?" I pressed.

"What?" he turned back to me.

"Well?"

"Well, what?"

"I canceled the bet."

"Nathan, you canceled my half of the bet, but I fully intend to have my team fuck your chocolate ass if your team loses."

"Why?"

"This is the perfect thing to motivate my guys. They've seen your sweet booty on the court, and they think it is mighty fine. I would love to see it and have a chance at it …" he let his words hang in the air.

"You want to see my ass? Now?"

Sam finished his beer and set the bottle down with a bang. "Sure." He looked at me with a hunger in his eyes.

"Right here?"

"No, we can go into the restroom. The bouncers don't start making their rounds until ten; we have time." He smiled and licked his lips.

Maybe this is what he needed to do to call off the bet. "Will you call off the bet?"

"Hmmm, I'll think about it. It depends on what you give me."

I stood up slowly, drained my beer bottle and headed to the men's room.

Sam jumped off his stool and followed close behind. His hand grabbed my butt and squeezed. "Nice and tight. Just how I love them."

I pushed the swinging door open and headed to the stall.

Sam followed and closed the door. He slid the bolt, not that it gave us any privacy. "Well?" he said.

I unbuckled my belt and unbuttoned my pants. As I unzipped, I watched Sam adjust his cock in his pants.

"Yeah, I'm getting hard," he said.

Despite the embarrassment, I was getting aroused, too. I opened my jeans and slipped them down to my knees.

His eyes worked over my cotton briefs, the white cotton contrasted against my mocha skin, and he stuck out his tongue.

My fingers dug under the waistband and stopped. I turned around and bent slightly forward.

"Wait," he said. "I want to savor this." He moved forward and caressed my ass. He kneaded my bubble butt and massaged it through the thin fabric. He slowly pulled my underwear down and exposed my brown booty.

"Beautiful," he said. His finger ran down my crease and slipped in between, searching for my hole. His tip found my dark pucker and explored.

My cheeks tensed up.

"Relax." His finger tickled me and sought entry, but I was too tight. He dropped to his knees and spread my cheeks. "Oh my, how caramelly sweet." He leaned in and licked my opening.

I jumped but spread my legs as wide as my jeans would allow and let him rim me. His tongue worked magic, sending pleasure over my body. My cock sprang to fully erect, and I stroked it.

He kissed me and sucked on me. His tongue drilled into the hole, seeking entry. Deeper and deeper it went.

I pushed back on his face, wanting him deeper inside me. His hand reached between my legs and grabbed my hairy balls. He squeezed them as his tongue worked deeper into me. He pulled down on my black nads.

He pulled back and sucked on one of his fingers. He slipped it between my cheeks and pressed into me. He wiggled it all the way in and tried to spread my sphincter as wide as it would go. He was rough.

"You've seen my ass, and you've tasted and poked it."

"And after I fuck it, we'll be done in here."

I stroked my thick cock a few more times, hoping that would help relax my ass.

Sam unzipped his pants and pulled out his cock.

"Not without a …"

"I picked one up on the way in."

I heard him rip the wrapper open and put on the condom. The freshly-opened and emptied packet of lube fell between my feet.

70

He moved closer to my ass and spread my cheeks wide.

I hoped this wouldn't take long.

He plunged in. His hairy balls slapped against my ass cheeks. His cock wasn't long or thick, so it went in easily. He humped me slowly at first and increased his speed. He reached around and grabbed my cock. "You have a huge one." His fingers wrapped around my shaft and jerked as he drilled into my ass.

I grabbed the bar on the wall to stabilize myself.

"That's it loser, take it, take it all." His free hand slapped my ass cheek, making it sting. He increased his speed. "Oh yeah, you're ass is tight." His jerked my cock, harder and harder.

Precum oozed out of the tip and lubricated the shaft as he jacked it.

His breathing came in short bursts. "I'm … gonna …" He grabbed my hips and plowed into me one last time and held his cock deep inside of me. He jerked my cock and despite the person, my cock shot out a thick load of cum. It hit the wall and slowly ran down the painted cinderblock.

He humped into me a few more times before he pulled out. He ripped the condom off his dick and tossed it into the toilet. "You're ass will be quite the prize."

And I heard a click behind me. I turned and saw he took a picture with his cell phone of my ass. One pearl of cream color cum glistened on my golden brown butt.

"My team is going to love this." He pressed a few buttons and then hit send.

I pulled some toilet paper off and wiped myself clean. As I pulled up my pants, I said, "So we're done. The bet is off."

"Hell no. That was the sweetest piece of ass I've had in a long time. My teammates are gonna love me, and they are going to love your bubble butt. More cushion for the pushing." He slapped my butt one more time.

"But you said ..."

"I said we'd be done in here, but I didn't say I was going to cancel the bet."

"You asshole."

"No, your asshole, in our locker room after our next game."

His cell phone beeped. He looked at the message. "They loved your picture. They can't wait to whoop your team's ass so they can fuck your booty."

I walked out of the bathroom and headed out of the Eagle. Tony, the captain of our team, smiled when he saw me and waved. "I'm glad you're here ..." he started.

"I'm not staying; I was just leaving." I slipped around him as he grabbed my arm.

"What's wrong?"

I spun around and saw Sam pointing and laughing at me.

"Nothing," I said. "Nothing." I pulled free from Tony and stormed out into the night.

Tony tried to call a few times that night, but I refused to pick up. The next few days went by as usual, and just before the big game, Coach Ryan finally caught me alone and asked, "So, what about the bet?"

"I called it off," I said.

"Good, I'm glad. It's not that we'd lose, but I can't have that kind of thing going on around here." He slapped my butt as I ran out of the locker room to the gym. "It looks bad for the league."

We lost.

Coach Ryan looked over at me and shook his head. Our team just fell apart; Sam's team played like they never played before, and they won by ten points.

Sweat ran down my face and burned my eyes. I pulled my basketball jersey up to wipe it away.

"Showing us what we won?" Sam called from across the court.

I pulled the shirt down and walked away. I'd wait until everyone was in the locker room, and then I'd slip away and join Sam's team to get this bet paid for, once and for all.

Tony ran after me. "He's such a jerk."

I continued on to the locker room and waited to disappear when no one was watching.

As I entered Sam's locker room, I saw his team was lined up along the bench that ran along the lockers. I looked down the row. The men grew in size the further I looked. Would I be able to survive all of their cocks? I stood in front of Sam.

"We've lined up by size," Sam said. "That way we won't stretch you out too fast."

"Let's just get this thing over with." I bent over the bench and pulled down my shorts. They dropped to my feet and I kicked them off. Spreading my legs, I readied my body. I felt a hand caress my ass cheeks and slipped under the elastic strap of my jock strap. He pulled it back and let it snap, like the boys did to girls with their training bras.

"Team, behold a beautiful booty. It's going to feel great to fuck that." He picked up the bottle of lube and poured it down my crack.

I could feel it run along my crease and down my hairy legs. "How much do you need?"

His finger followed the flow and paused at my hole. He circled my opening with his fingertip and started to push in. "It was tight before. Let's see if it still is." He bore his finger in to the first joint. "Oh, boy. He's tight. I'm glad I'm first."

I wouldn't be bragging about that small wiener, boy, I thought. My face burned from the embarrassment.

He stuck his finger all the way in and wiggled it back and forth, and not very gently, just like the last time. He pulled out of my ass, picked up a condom, and slipped it on. He lubed his dick and spread my cheeks. He grabbed my jock strap and pulled my hips to him.

I felt his cock slide up along my crease and rub along my sensitive pucker. He sought entry with his mushroom tip, but my ass tensed up.

"Relax, this won't hurt much at all." He laughed and slapped my ass cheek. "Hey guys. It's going to be a long night."

The locker room door burst open, and I tried to see who was coming in to witness my humiliation.

Tony rounded the row of lockers and commanded, "Stop right there."

I started to stand up, but Sam pushed me back down. "Stay."

Tony approached and pointed at Sam. "You can stop right now."

Sam let go and stepped in front of me, his little cock sticking straight out in front of him. "What are you doing here? You're team lost the bet, and now, we're collecting."

"That's why we're here. We lost as a team, and we're going to pay as a team." Tony gently moved Sam away and took my arm. He pulled me to him and hugged me. "Thanks for the sacrifice, but we're here now, you're not taking it for the team."

I saw my whole team lined up behind Tony, and they all nodded at me.

"You guys don't need to be here. I made the bet. I'll pay."

"You made the bet for us, and we lost. So we're willing to do this for you. You're part of the team, win or lose." Tony turned to the rest of the team. "Line up you guys and drop your shorts." He looked over at the winning team. "Okay guys, pick which one you want and assume the position."

Sam moved over to me.

Tony cock blocked him. "He's not for you. You're all mine."

"Tony ..."

"Nathan, trust me on this." Tony motioned for someone to come over. It was Neil.

Neil moved over to me and smiled as his face turned pink.

"Did you do this? Did you tell Tony about the bet?" Nathan reached out and touched his chest. He had a crush on Neil for the longest time, but had always been afraid to ask him out.

"Sam was being such an asshole about the bet; I figured I had to do something. When you rushed out of the Eagle that night, Tony found me and asked if I knew what was going on."

I leaned forward and kissed him.

Neil stood stock still for a moment and then grabbed me and pulled me into his arms. His mouth devoured mine, and our tongues tasted each other.

His hands worked down my back and squeezed my bare ass.

A couple of guys were getting to know each other on one side, as Tony and Sam got to business.

My erection strained against my jock and sought his.

Neil brushed his pelvis against mine, and I could feel his hard-on. We rubbed up and down, our shafts dueling.

I looked down the bench and saw my teammates bent over, their asses in the air. Sam's team worked my team's asses, and I felt guilty.

Neil sensed a change in my mood and kissed me. "I'm here, and I want you. If you'll have me." His lips brushed against mine softly. "You don't have to do this if you don't want to."

I looked into his deep blue eyes and knew, Yes, I wanted him. Now.

Tony waited for Sam to slip on his condom. "What's wrong?" Tony's perfect, hairy ass stared Sam in the face, and I could see how dark his skin was and the beautiful pelt of fur that covered each cheek. My hard-on grew from the amazing sight.

"I can't get …"

Tony spread his cheeks wider and looked at him, waiting for him to get hard.

I removed my jersey and set it on the bench. Neil slipped his shorts down, and I gasped at his bulging jock strap. A thick bush of hair escaped from the waistband, and two hairy balls along with a massive cock stretched the mesh-like pocket to see through. His shaft was thick, and I worried he rip me wide open. "I'm tight."

Neil slipped off his jock, and his cock slapped his torso as it sprang up. Sweat and precum sprayed across my ass, warm and wet. "I'll be gentle." He slipped on his condom and lubed himself well.

I remembered how much Sam's little dick hurt and tensed my ass.

"Relax," Neil said as he lubed my crease. He worked more lube into my hole and gently stretched me. No pain, only a warm pleasure. He inserted two fingers and then three. Oiling and lubing, working my tight muscle to want more, crave his cock.

And it did. My sphincter released, and Neil knew it. He lubed his cock one more time and slid his nine inches up and down my crack. His thick tip teased my hole and stimulated all my nerves. He slowly inserted the mushroom head and rocked back and forth.

I pushed back against him, urging him to fill me.

His hands grasped my hips as he guided himself deeper in. The fat head of his cock strained for a second and then released. The rest of his shaft flowed inside me as a warm pleasure flooded me.

My legs threatened to collapse as his balls hit my bubble butt.

Shane's ass was being plugged by Sam's center. Their center was a seven-foot black man with the biggest dick I had ever seen. Shane rode it hard, as sweat poured down his face. He groaned with every thrust.

I looked over to see how Tony and Sam were doing. Sam ripped his condom off his flaccid cock and stormed off to the shower room.

Tony caught me watching and smiled. He stood up and moved over to me and kissed me. He turned and faced Neil. "Thanks for telling me." He moved forward and kissed Neil.

Neil rocked back and forth inside me as he kissed Tony.

I looked up, and Tony's cock strained against his red jock. I reached up and freed his balls. They hung down low and were heavy, swinging back and forth.

Neil saw what I was doing and slowly pulled out of my ass. He motioned for me to flip over onto my back on the bench; now there was more room.

I lay down on the wood as he repositioned himself between my legs.

He reinserted his monster cock, as Tony straddled the bench. His balls hovered over my mouth. Neil pulled Tony's face to him, and they kissed as he drilled his cock deeper into me.

I stretched my neck, so I could pull one of Tony's balls into my mouth. He shaved them. They were pink and perfect, and one slipped in easily. I sucked on it and drew down on it.

Tony moaned with pleasure in Neil's mouth.

Skin slapping and men moaning with pleasure filled the locker room. The smell of urine, male sweat and unwashed jock straps was masked by the raw scent of man on man sex.

I guided Tony's other testicle to my lips and swallowed it, too.

Tony sat down so his balls could go down my throat. His asshole came down on my nose.

I inhaled deeply and savored the sweaty taste and musky smell, as my body tingled from pleasure of Neil's cock. I reached up and freed Tony's cock from the pouch and watched as it bounced up and down as I worked on his balls. Precum oozed out of the tip and ran along the underside of his shaft. I milked more out of him and soon tasted the sweet nectar.

Neil increased his speed in my ass. His cock seemed to have thickened and filled me more. His deep strokes filled me and brushed against my prostate gland, sending pre-orgasmic shivers through my balls and shaft.

Tony guided my head back and slowly inserted his eight-inch cock into my mouth. He reached over and pinched Neil's nipples.

I felt like a spit roast between these two men's cocks.

Moans and groans of pleasure echoed throughout the locker room as the other pairs enjoyed their workout. But Neil and Tony's bodies demanded my full attention, and I forgot the other team members were even there.

Tony's cock drooled sweet precum into my mouth and added to my saliva.

I sucked harder on his cock as he quickened his pace. I tipped my head back and allowed my throat to open to take his full length all the way down. His balls bounced against my eyes as he humped my face.

Tony's testicles were full and ripe after the game. He always needed to blow a load after a game.

Neil filled my ass and pounded into me faster and harder.

My back slipped on the wooden bench ping-ponging my body between the two men's cocks. I could feel the pressure build in my balls, and I started stroking my dick. Precum oozed out and lubed my shaft, making it easier to jack off.

Two couples became a foursome, and it was difficult to tell where one stopped and the other one started.

Neil and Tony kissed again and looked down at me. "Maybe this bet was a great idea after all," Tony said.

Neil continued to pound my ass. "I'm glad I got you."

My balls started to rise up, and my sucking on Tony's cock increased.

"I'm gonna come," Tony said.

My hand rose up and stroked his dick as it slipped in and out of my mouth.

His balls pulled up tight along the side of his shaft, and the first wave exploded down my throat.

I swallowed and breathed, almost choking on his load, but as the next orgasm hit, I drew down harder on him.

His balls emptied into me. What I couldn't swallow oozed out and dripped down the side of my face.

Neil quickened his pace and grabbed my cock. He stroked in rhythm of his thrusts. "I'm close," he gasped.

Tony's cock pulled out of my mouth, and I swallowed again. "Me, too." My pleasure took over, and my balls spasmed hard. Cum shot out of my dick and filled Neil's hand. The thick, hot load lubed my cock and sent orgasm after orgasm over my body.

Neil's body tensed, and he slammed hard into my butt. He pressed in harder and held it there, as his balls emptied. He strained forward and continued to press into me deeper. He fell on top of me, my load making it easy for him to slip back and forth over my cock. Another wave of cum came out of me, and my whole body shuttered.

Tony sat down by my head and combed through my hair as we relaxed. He smiled down at me and said. "Wow, you can bet your black ass any time you want."

Neil rode up and shook his head. "Not anymore, this booty is my booty." He slowly withdrew, sending more waves of pleasure through me.

Tony helped me sit up. "Maybe we should hit the showers."

We watched as the other couples continued.

I stood up and grabbed their hands. "Let's go. I'm sure we'll have even more fun cleaning up, and I'll bet my black ass on that one."

Neil slapped it. "That's my ass, but I may share with Tony." And we hit the shower room.

DREAM LOVER
By Landon Dixon

Malcolm was sleeping, flat on his back on the bed, head turned to the right side on the pillow, sheet drawn up to his chin. My balls stirred with desire, the dark, handsome guy looking so peaceful and innocent, fucking hot.

Malcolm and I had been going together for only a couple of months. But he'd already given me his key. And I'd used it, to let myself in early that morning. To observe the luscious licorice man sleeping. It's a fetish I have, watching men sleep, kissing them, licking them, fondling them, fucking them while they sleep. A man's never so beautiful than when he's at peace with the world, nestled in the warm, comforting arms of slumber.

I hadn't mentioned my mancolepsy to Malcolm. This was my first chance to give him a try.

I slipped off my T-shirt, kicked off my shoes, and unbuckled my jeans and pushed them down and off. I stepped out into the warm, yellow early-morning glow of Malcolm's bedroom completely naked, my cock stretched rock-hard in front of me, gleaming dark and smooth and long as my boyfriend's body stretched undercover out on the bed.

I gripped shaft and buckled at the knees, suppressing a moan, my meat throbbing wildly in my palm. I stroked, caressing snake, watching the perfect rising and falling of Malcolm's chest, the twin points of his nipples indenting the thin cotton sheet, the rigid outline of his form.

Savoring the exquisite moment, I jacked slow and sure and strong, slipped a hand up onto my chest, clasped fingers around a stiffened nipple and rolled. I had to swallow another groan of pleasure, pulling on my cock, pulling on my nipple. I plucked at the another nipple, got that black bud up and brimming, then slid my free hand down my body and around my erection and onto my balls.

I cupped and squeezed and twisted my shaven sack, tugging on my smooth-skinned dong. I almost bent double under the illicit sexual pressure, working the nuts, the pole. And then I advanced, cock leading the way.

The shag hid my footsteps. I stood right next to the bed, cock jutting out in the warm, breathless air, straining to overshadow Malcolm's calm, chiseled face. I reached out and gripped the top of the sheet, drew it slowly down.

More and more of the lean, muscled man appeared, the white curtain lowering on his ebony body, sliding down his chest, popping over his nipples. I stared at those blue-black buds and licked my lips, almost tasting their thick, rubbery firmness.

Malcolm's arms were down by his sides, and as I pulled the sheet lower, over his flat, hard, undulating stomach, he clenched at the edges, grabbing onto the reinforced cotton. "Damn," I breathed, stopped just above his bellybutton.

I knew the guy slept in the buff, but the way his hips were turned slightly, his cock wasn't even a bulge in the sheet. I had to do something about that. If I couldn't see it, I could feel it.

I climbed onto the bed, slowly, carefully, stealthily, a spring-whisperer extraordinaire. There was hardly any sound at all. Just the smooth, uninterrupted breathing of my man, the pounding of my heart in my chest and the beating of the blood in my cock.

I straddled Malcolm's narrow waist, standing up on my knees, not touching the sleeping dawg. My cock speared out over him, and I gave it a few brisk, loving tugs, feeling the heat of Malcolm's body so close, smelling the musky scent of the hot-blooded man.

His nipples were just too good to resist. I lowered my silky fingers and softly traced circles around the pebbled areolas, as delicate as twin feathers. Malcolm smacked his lips and thrust his chin up, arched his muscle-humped chest. But his eyelids stayed firmly closed. I lowered my head in place of my fingers and slid out the glistening pink length of my tongue and tapped one of Malcolm's buds with the tip.

He grunted, his night-shaded nipples swelling up thicker, higher. I tickled the other pointed protuberance with my tongue, breathing hot, humid breath all over it. Then I withdrew my sticker and pushed out my lips, softly kissing one of the buds, the other, cushioning a nipple between my lips and oh-so-gently tugging.

Another grunt, a turn of the head. I nursed on Malcolm's other nipple. The pair soon shone wet and rigid with my loving. I nipped one with my teeth and then drew back. Something else had swelled up now – in between Malcolm's legs.

I cautiously kneed my way up higher on the bed, almost over top Malcolm's head. Then I lifted my right leg, swung it around, rotating my body. My left knee slid onto the pillow next to Malcolm's slumbering head, right knee planting down on the other side.

It was a delicate maneuver, but I'm a pretty delicate guy; except for that swelled-up appendage in between my legs, of course. I let it hang down to Malcolm's face, bloated hood taking the warm, even breath from his mouth. As I faced his own swelling cock in the sheet.

He'd moved his hips flat now, so that I could clearly see his outlined dick trailing down his right thigh. I knew just how big that member could get, and I vowed to get it up and coursing full-length, as my man slept.

I traced a finger over the thin cotton, from the base of Malcolm's cock to the tip. I could feel the rugged veins and the meat of the shaft, the lip and thickness of the hood, all through my finger and up my arm and into my dick. Malcolm caressed my cap with his heated exhalations, his cock twitching, expanding, as I finger-stroked up and down.

One finger quickly wasn't enough to encapsulate all of the ballooning dong. I leant it a hand, grasping shaft through sheet, feeling the pulse, the heft, pumping warm and damp and even. Malcolm sighed and thrust his hips upwards, his beefy cock filling my clutching, shifting hand.

The big guy was as easily aroused as I was and when aroused, even bigger. His prick surged out down his thigh, stretching long and meaty under my moving hand. I had him stroked out to his full fearsome potent potential in a matter of moments, his cock consciously taking what his mind could only dream about.

I gripped his dong with both hands and squeezed, lowering my hips so that my raging cock kissed parted lips with mushroomed hood. Malcolm stuck out his tongue, wetting his lips, and my slit. I barely caught the moan in my throat. Then I kissed Malcolm's massive cap through the sheet, French-style.

He gave voice to what I was feeling – a groan of pleasure. Still asleep, but so awake and alert between his legs. I gripped his dick at the wide base and licked up and down the tree trunk shaft, bumping my own hood up and down on Malcolm's cushioning lips.

His hot breath flooded my groin, faster now. I curled my lips around the swollen, sheeted bulge of his cap and sucked gently through the threads. As I dipped hood into Malcolm's partially-open mouth, shuddering when I hit wet tongue.

His mouth opened up wider, to make room for his breathing and my cockhead. I lowered half my cap inside, the silky slide of his lips, the hot, damp touch of his tongue, making me quiver all over. I held onto his wood for dear life, daring to go deeper, sinking my entire hood inside his mouth and then basking in the wet-velvet heat.

His mouth closed on my cap, lips sealing, sucking.

"Fuck!" I groaned.

The guy had taken to my cockhead like a baby to a mother's nipple. He was still asleep, but he was sucking on my hood. I slid my lips up and down his dong, giving him the best blowjob I could under the covered circumstances. My body and brain burned with the awesome eroticism of it all, that earnest pull on the tip of my cock.

It couldn't last. I couldn't last. It had gone even further than I'd imagined, even given my fine-tuned skills as a sexual dream-weaver.

But it was Malcolm who went off first. His cock jumped under my stroking lips and swabbing tongue, the tremendous shaft surging cum-hard – the cock coming. Semen spurted out, staining the sheet, burst after burst, Malcolm pumping out his unconscious ecstasy. My head went even dizzier, tasting the shooting sperm through the cotton, smelling the heated ball juice. My own cock jerked, and a shudder of sheer delight ran the length of my trembling body.

I just managed to pop my top free of Malcolm's plush lips and shift my cock over, using the last quivering ounce of my willpower. So that my jets of joy splashed the pillow, didn't drown the guy in a heated sea of jizz.

The only thing tougher than getting Malcolm and myself off while he slept, was getting that bed linen off and washed clean before he woke up.

#####

It was a dream, a warm, lush, beautiful dream. I was in Malcolm's bed. Malcolm was caressing my bare butt cheeks with his strong, wide-palmed hands, spooning in behind me. He was naked. I was naked. His smooth, rubbing palms and long, stroking fingers felt so very good on the tingling skin of my buttocks.

"Yes," I moaned, thrusting out my mounded backside.

Malcolm cupped the packed pair, squeezed them, his hot breath filling my ear. He licked in behind my ear, and I shuddered, shivering my cheeks in his hands.

"Frot me, big guy," I murmured.

He bit into my earlobe, liking the idea. But I liked his idea just as much.

Because he squirmed down behind me in the bed, got butt-level, his face facing my ass. His hands spread my cheeks and his tongue shot in to fill the gap, stroke my crack all wet and wonderful and wickedly sensuous.

I jerked with pure delight, the damp, budded sensation of his tongue on the tender skin of my butt cleavage amazing. He licked again, and again, lapping my crack, tonguing me from balls to tailbone, over and over.

My cock boned out full-length, vibratingly erect. Each long, moist tongue-stroke flooded shimmering heat all through my body. And when Malcolm corkscrewed the tip of his mouthorgan all around my pucker, I knew I was in heaven.

We hadn't done much ass play in our relationship so far. But to sleep is perchance to dream.

Malcolm proved an expert in the art of eating ass. He squirmed his slippery sticker all around my manhole. Then he pushed and pulled my cheeks as wide as he could manage, really opening me up, thrusting his tongue right inside, plugging me full of erotic pleasure. He hardened his tongue into a pink blade and jabbed it in and out, fucking my anus.

I undulated my bottom, taking it and loving it. Malcolm poked deeper, filling my chute, his tongue wet and hot and alive inside me, plunging me to a whole new depth of sexual sensation.

I groaned with despair when he finally, slowly drew his sticker back out of my ass. But he quickly filled the void, squirming back up in behind me and sliding his slab of beef into the slickened chasm of my butt cleavage. I moaned, his massive dong cramming up between my cheeks, gliding along the oversensitized skin of my butt crack.

He was pronged out as long and thick as his huge tool would go, I could feel it, all through my ass and body. He let go of my cheeks, spilling the tingling flesh over his dick, locking his cock down tight. I gripped it even tighter with my buttocks, reveling in the wicked sensation of all that dong lodged along my ass crack, pumping my bum cleavage.

This was one wild dream, brought on by our torrid night of lovemaking earlier, no doubt. Malcolm gripped my shoulders and pumped his hips, frotting back and forth in my crack. I blazed with passion, my ass on fire, the slide of the man's massive sledge between my cheeks simply awesome.

Malcolm and I had never gone anal before. "Fuck my ass, Malcolm," I breathed now. "Pull that huge dong of yours out of my crack and stick it in my ass. Fuck me!" In dreams, anything was possible.

Malcolm swirled his tongue around in my ear, shunted his cock in my crack. Before pulling back, out. I spasmed when I felt the cool mist of lube, shivered when I felt Malcolm's fingers smoothing the slipperiness into my cleavage, smearing it all around my pucker. I held my breath.

Bloated hood bumped up against my manhole. "Yes, Malcolm! Stick me! Fuck me!"

His grunt came loud and clear and dripping with lust in my ear. His cap pressed harder against my starfish, squished through, in, busting my ring and bursting into my anus. I bit my lip, trembling body and soul.

He pressed his advantage home, breathing hard, squeezing his ebony snake into my chute. Inch after swollen inch plowed inside my ass, stretching my walls and blowing my subconscious mind. My butt swelled with cock, my body with electric sensation.

"Fuck, I'm buried inside you! Balls to the booty!" Malcolm hissed in my ear.

He didn't have to tell me. I could feel every engorged, throbbing inch of his powerful prick, stuffing my ass and my dreams. "Fuck me, Malcolm!" I pleaded.

His hands went damp on my shoulders, his breath coming in gasps, his body burning against mine. We were joined in the most intimate, manly manner possible – at the cock and chute. Malcolm shifted his hips, pumping my anus.

I pushed back, helping the man along, helping him saw my ass with his log. "Fuck!" he grunted, feeling it almost as much as I did.

The bed creaked, we groaned, the pressure building and building. It felt like my ass would explode with all of that cock surging back and forth, hammering away at my backdoor. My own cock jutted out from my loins, brimming with feeling, and precum. Malcolm reached around and gripped it, ripped it, pumping in rhythm to his own cock pumping my anus.

It felt so real, so intense. My balls boiled, my butt ablaze, my cock about to explode.

I blinked my eyes open. Just as Malcolm yelled, "Fuck! I'm gonna come!" He yanked on my cock, pounding into my chute from behind.

It was no dream! It was really happening! The full radical realization of it dawned on me. Just as I jerked, spurted semen out of my hand-jacked cock. As Malcolm spasmed, shot white-hot sperm deep into my bowels.

I stared unblinking at the morning sun-glowed curtains, blasting blistering orgasm out of my ruptured cock, taking sizzling orgasm up my reamed ass from Malcolm's detonated dong.

The guy later confessed it'd always been a fantasy of his to make love to a man while he slept. He hoped I wasn't too upset by his imposing on me like that?

Who says dreams don't come true?

SECOND HELPINGS
By Don Mika

"I can't believe I was begging for this stupid job just a week ago," I mumbled, collecting an array of abandoned silverware and heaps of unfinished food. I shook my head in anger thinking of the things my friends were doing with their summers: my best friend, Wolf, away at basketball camp, and constantly calling me to tell me what fun he was having, and what pro athletes he had met. Then there was Conner and Cameron, the rich set of twins, whose family always spent the summer seeing Europe. I was willing to bet they weren't dropping fries for extra cash.

As far as crumby jobs go, I have to say mine was the worse. Hamburger Haven – doesn't the name just say it all? Even if I weren't a vegetarian, I could find a million reasons to hate this place. For starters, the silly, plastic, oversized hamburger, which bobs up and down on the hat. Sometimes I feel it bobbing hours after I've gone home and taken the uniform off. I call it phantom bobbing. I swear I feel that weight of that silly patty in my sleep.

Why did my mother's dream have to be to own a diner? If I had only been born into the family that owned the ice-cream parlor across town, the uniform would be something that I don't have to run to the back to hide each time a person from school comes in, which is often. I would even settle for being heir to the small coffee shop down the street, even though it is going out of business. At least, their uniforms are tasteful: khaki pants and a classic, blue, button-down shirt.

What is it about the colors orange, red, and yellow that are supposed to increase appetites? Looking at these uniforms and loud walls always has just the opposite effect on me.

"I'll be finished in about three minutes." The voice came from a guy in the far right of the diner. He must have been eyeing the clock just as I had and seen that it was past our closing time. If not, he got the less than subtle hint when my co-worker, Debra, walked over to the door and switched the neon sign from open to closed.

"Take your time, sugar," she said, continuing to clear tables, but flashed me a warning sign to be on guard. She always got nervous when it was time to lock up.

I stopped to check my image in the shiny, metallic tray I carried, hoping that Debra wouldn't see me. She always gave me a hard time about being so into my looks.

"Will you be okay if I leave a little early?" she whispered to me, still flashing our last customer leery eyes as he practically choked himself with handfuls of our secret recipe fries. "The babysitter called a few minutes ago, and I promised her that I would be back early tonight. I've already done most of the cleaning, 'cept a few pots and pans. I'll make it up to you tomorrow; I swear."

"No need. Like you said, you've already done the bulk of the work." I was fuming inside from being left with extra work, but I wanted my chance to be alone with the stranger. Something about him told me that he was someone I should get to know better.

"Thanks a million, honey." She gave me a kiss and doubled back to loudly announce that she had already emptied out the drawer, and given all the petty cash to my mother. That, I was sure, was done to let our late eater know that he was barking up the wrong tree if he had plans to rob us.

I felt secure that that had not been his motive for staying late. I had caught him checking out my ass in the tight uniform pants, more than once, as I walked by him. I wasn't sure if I was correct the first time, so I began to make special trips around his area, bending over to refill napkin trays and rake crumbs from the loud, orange benches. All the while, his eyes stayed fixed on me, his hand adjusting his manhood under the table.

Now that Debra was gone, I playfully busied myself with straightening the furniture, giving him a view of my skinny, round ass with each chair I lifted onto the abandoned tables. He never took his eyes off me but continued to eat in silence.

"So, what's your name?" I finally brought myself to ask, figuring that he was too far on the down low to allow himself the first move.

"They call me Keeto." He wiped his mouth with a graceful mannerism, not suiting such a thuggish specimen, and flashed me a smile that was covered with a gold grill, my weakness. "I've been waiting for you to ask all night."

"Oh yeah? Why didn't you just come over and tell me? You certainly don't look like the shy type to me." I flashed him all thirty-two of my perfectly white teeth. I was turning on all the charms, as I was sure I had him in my clutches now, silly ass hamburger hat or not.

"I knew you would come to me," he bragged. "I saw it in your eyes. Plus, they say that good things come to those who wait. You looked like you were worth waiting for."

"And what if I hadn't come to you? What if it had been me to leave first instead of my friend? Would you have followed me, or would you still be in here, shooting these same smooth lines to her?"

"Did you hear me order any fish?" He gave me a deep, raspy chuckle. "Nah, homey; I ain't one of those confused cats that play both sides of the fence. I figured out that pussy wasn't my thing a long time ago."

Usually, his revelation would have been a turn-off to me. At only eighteen, I was just young and naïve enough to believe that no completely gay man could possess the machismo that I desired. I had always opted for married men, bi-curious guys, or men who just didn't give a fuck as long as they got off, but there was something intriguingly macho about Keeto. I had noticed the swagger in his walk when he came in, the raw, animalistic way he ate his food, and the lustful look in his eyes as he stared me up and down and licked his lips.

His hungry stare had made me wish that I could wave a wand and make everybody else disappear so that he could have his way with me. Judging from the way he ate, I had no doubt that he would have been forceful and unyielding, the way I loved it. That thought had my hole opening and closing in anticipation as I stared into his almond-shaped, hazel eyes.

"Well, Mr. Keeto, aren't you ever going to ask my name?" I teased.

"You'll tell me when the time is right," he shot back cockily.

"Oh, will I? And when will that be?"

"The next time we kiss."

"That's funny. What makes you think that we're going to …?

My words stifled as he stood and pulled me towards him. I could feel his muscular chest and stomach move against mine. I could feel his semi-erect manhood poking at my thigh through the fabric of his baggy sweats. One of his hands walked from my shoulders, down my back, and unto my ass. His other hand locked behind my neck and pulled my face closer to his. His lips met mine, and the part of my mind that told me to pull away and play hard to get was silenced.

Even with the added taste of cheeseburger and fries, his was the sweetest pair of lips I had ever tasted. I nearly cried when he pulled them free of mine. My body weakened by the feel of his strong embrace, and I swayed as he let me down (I had been standing on my tiptoes because he was a good six feet and two inches, while I was only five-seven). My breathing became guttural as his body grazed mine one last time. He looked at the clock and then abruptly turned to leave.

"No … wait!" I called after him. "Keeto!" I ran to the door and stepped outside, but I didn't see any signs of him. Seemingly, he had vanished in thin air. I didn't even hear the hum of a car in the distance.

# # # # #

"Are you okay?" Uncle June yelled at me over the bustle of metal trays being heaped into the sink. "You've been moping around here like a dog that just got fixed for weeks now!"

"Not a wound on the bodies. No signs of a struggle. Just dead." My cousin, Crystal, was following him around with the newspaper as he moved through the kitchen. "It's the damndest thing, Daddy! They can't figure out how these people are dying, but they're almost certain it's the same sicko killing them."

"That's nice, baby!" He continued to ignore her and focused on me again. "What the hell is your problem?"

"I'm okay," I sighed, and pushed the greasy pan into which I had been repeatedly scratching Keeto's name into the water before June could see it.

I couldn't get Keeto off my mind. I saw his handsome smile in my sleep and fantasized about his olive brown skin roaming my body each night before drifting off. I spent my time in the shower thinking about running my fingers through his silky afro and of having him tangle his manly fingers in my dreadlocks. I kept imagining what delights awaited me beneath his baggy clothes, but mostly, I thought about his burger flavored kiss and the smell of his cologne as he held me next to him. Had he actually been wearing cologne, or could I have only been attracted to the raw pheromones in his manly sweat? Either way, I was intoxicated and enticed.

I lost my appetite and my will to do anything but think about the next time we would meet. I wanted the chance to tell him my name. I couldn't understand why three weeks had passed with no sign of him. I had certainly been looking. I had taken to closing the diner each night, though it was a usually despised task. I knew that if I ever saw him again, it would be on a late night, like the one on which we had met. My efforts proved fruitless.

"Welcome back, stranger!" I heard Debra call from the front of the diner.

Could she have been talking to my Keeto?

I rushed from the kitchen, forgetting that my soapy hands were full of plates, until I heard the sound of several crashing to the floor. All eyes in the diner locked on me, and none belonged to Keeto. Debra had been talking to an elderly guy, whom we had assumed dead when he stopped his nightly visits.

"What the hell is wrong with you?" asked Crystal, coming out of the kitchen with a tray of nachos. "All these nights of closing up late getting to you? You look sick, baby! You been acting loco for days now!"

"I'm just fine," I lied.

"Go on home!" Uncle June fussed, snatching the remaining plates from my hands. "Get some sleep and come back tomorrow ... only if you feel better."

"I can't do that, Uncle June. Really, I am fine."

"I wasn't making a suggestion, boy! That was an order. Crystal and I will lock up tonight. I don't want to see you no more until three o'clock tomorrow; you got that?"

"Fine!" I took the keys from my waistband and threw them over the counter. The burger on the stupid hat made a squeaky noise as I made it follow the keys. I flung my apron to the ground, and walked out without even acknowledging Debra and Crystal's goodbyes.

As my feet angrily pounded the sidewalk, I thought about how silly I was being. Why was I sulking because I had missed a chance to wait for somebody who was almost certain not to show? I decided that I would take my uncle's advice and get the sleep I so badly needed. I would wake with a clear mind and no more thoughts of Keeto. As far as I was concerned, Keeto was nothing more than a distant memory, which I would do my best to make fade fast.

I meant every word of that promise, but as soon as I had turned the corner that connected the ally to Mom's diner, there sat Keeto, perched on the ragged fence. My heart sped on sight, and I made my feet do the same thing. I walked right past, giving him the treatment he had given me for nearly three weeks.

"Oh, so you don't see me?" he chuckled.

"No, I don't see you!" I continued to walk.

"Tesmond, wait!" he called behind me, and that stopped me dead in my tracks, wondering how he knew my name when I had never told it to him. I spun around, and he was standing face to face with me, though I had been yards ahead of him. How could I have not heard his footsteps if he had run to catch up with me, and how the hell could he have done so in a split second?

"Who the hell are you, and what do you want from me?" I asked.

"Love," he smiled, ignoring my first question. "All I want to do is love you." He pulled me closer to him, and I decided that his answer was good enough.

"Where the hell have you been?" I demanded. I began to cry as I cursed him and unleashed the anxiety that had built in me over the weeks.

"Shhh!" His lulling sound caused all my fury to go away. It seemed as if I had no choice but to be silent. Even my tears ceased to fall from my eyes. I straightened up, as if I hadn't been falling apart just seconds earlier. I no longer could recall why I had even been upset.

The way that he held me made me suddenly feel the need to feel his name fall off my tongue. "Keeto," I breathed, burying my face in the serenity of his chest. He wore no cologne, but his body odor was surprisingly sweet and refreshing, even in the humid weather that made my sweaty clothes cling to me, reeking of a day's work. He kissed my forehead, and I raised my head to taste his lips, which were even sweeter than I could remember from the last time we'd shared an embrace. His strong arms pulled me even closer into him. Sliding his hands down my back in a way that sent electric pulses through my very being, he finally found my ass, moist and sweaty from the summer walk. He didn't seem to mind the perspiration.

I could feel his loins throb against my own as his hands cupped my buttocks, pulling my cheeks apart with a lustful roughness that rivaled my own savage urges. I wrapped my legs around his waist and felt myself produce jets of precum as he slid his pulsing lump back and forth against mine. For a minute, I forgot that we were still fully dressed. The alley and the threat of us being seen by anyone, namely Uncle June, if he ventured out to dump the garbage, disappeared.

Still kissing me and pawing savagely at my back, Keeto walked me over to a row of dumpsters and sat me down on the only one that had a lid. I was too engulfed in the moment, and too turned on by the man I was with, to be disgusted by the smell of spoiled meat products. I couldn't stop humping against him, and I wouldn't allow him to pull free from our lip lock, making his attempts at pulling down my pants clumsy and laborious.

After several minutes of me fighting against it, he freed himself from my lips, allowing his own to walk down my neck. He ripped my shirt over my head and lapped at my nipples with his tongue. That was followed by a tug at each with his front teeth. The sensation caused another jet of precum to escape the hole in the throbbing head of my cock. My asshole began to twitch and pucker in anticipation of what was to come next, but it seemed as if it would be a while before I would get to feel Keeto inside of me. He was slowly teasing my stomach with his tongue, seductively tracing my belly button. The threat of us being seen by anybody passing by seemed to turn both of us on.

"You ready?" he asked, ripping my pants down to my ankles.

"I've been ready since the first time I saw you," I shamelessly admitted.

"I hope I don't disappoint you."

I knew that there was no possible way that Keeto could not live up to my expectations. I had felt that monstrous cock strain through his stretch pants, pushing against mine, teasing my hole through my sweaty uniform pants, making me ache to feel him tunnel into depths that no other lover had achieved. The mere thought had me so excited that I was literally moments away from exploding.

I slid further down on the can, making my shuttering hole more accessible to him. He pushed my thighs up and lapped at the twitching circle with his tongue. He gently tugged at the surrounding patch of hair with his teeth, and I winced in discomfort. The feel of his tongue burrowing inside of me made that discomfort fade as quickly as it had come.

"OOOH YESS!" I hissed, closing my eyes. What he was doing to my insides was completely unfathomable. I had never imagined that a human tongue could drill so deeply into the anal cavity, but Keeto's was making me feel as if a giant, slick penis was inside me, gently sliding across my prostate.

Even more exciting than the actual sensation of being internally teased, was the feel of his hands on my ass: rough, purposeful, intent, and uncompromising. Those massive, soft hands stretched my cheeks to the threat of tearing, pulling me unto his face, making the supple flesh of my ass jiggle and vibrate against his mouth while he produced savage slurping noises and groaned his approval of the taste and smell. It seemed as if he would tear me into halves to get better access to my sweet hole, and that beastly passion turned me on in ways that I can't verbalize. I wanted him to take me with the same intensity that he orally serviced me.

Suddenly, I grew so excited that I literally got frightened. My heart raced and my body ran boiling hot. Electricity seemed to course through every inch of me, especially my leaking cock. My ass contracted around his tongue and opened up over and over again. I tightened my thighs around his head, attempting to stop him from going any further. "Stop, Keeto!" I begged, though the sensation he was giving was nothing short of pleasurable. "Please stop, baby!"

He ignored my request, determined not to give up until he had made my body succumb to whatever it was he wanted to achieve. His moans of pleasure grew into animalistic growls, and his saliva trickled more freely into my hole. The teasing sensation of his lips sucking my rim also intensified, as did his variation of forcing his tongue into the pouting opening.

"Please Keeto!" I begged, shaking all over in delight. I had never even had a full orgasm, induced by the manipulation of my penis, feel so intense, but there I lay, eyes nailed shut, trembling, toes curled heavenward, from only having my anus teased. "OOOOOH SHIT! OOOOOOOOOOOOOOOOH OOOW FUUCK! KEETO, OOOOOOOOOH, KEETO!"

He pushed my hands away from my exploding cock as I attempted to stop the flood. His tongue lapped at the waterfall of sperm as it rushed from my tip in seemingly endless jets. The chills and the intensity were almost too much to bear, so pleasurable that it seemed dangerous. Never had I had, nor had I witnessed, an orgasm last so long.

"Damn, Keeto! What did you do to me?" I gnashed, clawing at the sides of the trashcan until my fingers turned white from the pressure. My body still shook uncontrollably, and my asshole violently opened and closed, pushing out the surplus of spit he had packed in with the same force that sperm was rushing from my penis. "Hold me, Keeto! Please, baby, hold me!" I begged, genuinely frightened that I was going to come myself to death.

My desperate moans seemed to make him snap out of his ass-eating trance. He stood and looked at me with a guilty face. It seemed as if he had actually been harming me and regretted his actions. He pulled me into a hug, and the moment that my chest came into contact with his, the chills from the orgasm stopped, as did the flow of semen. Only a few droplets trailed off my tip and rushed down my thighs.

"Let's get you home," he said, helping me down from the dumpster. I was still so lightheaded from the orgasm that he had to redress me.

"Wait," I protested, still anxious to feel him inside of me, or to at least know the delight of having his huge cock invade my mouth. "Let me please you back, baby. Come on; after that, you have to let me make you feel good, too."

"Next time," he promised.

I didn't know why, but he seemed deeply saddened as he walked with me. When we reached my doorstep, I stared into his face, begging him to follow me in. He refused, turning to head off in the opposite direction. I strained to see him in the darkness, but, seemingly, as soon as he had left my porch, he had vanished into the thick fog and the misty raindrops that had just started to fall.

Had I seen tears on his face? No. I told myself that they had only been raindrops. Guys as hardcore as my Keeto didn't cry, but I couldn't deny sensing a deep sadness within him as we walked. Besides, we had been under the shelter of my porch when the rain started.

And had he been leading the way as we walked? How could that have been; he had never been to my house? I had been too giddy to notice it before, but, with no instructions from me, he had led me right to my doorstep.

"Who are you, Keeto?" I breathed, sticking my key in the weathered lock. As I thought back to how he had also known my name without having been told, and to the sensations he had given me earlier, I began to think that my question should have been what was he. Either way, I was aching to find out more about my mystery lover, no matter how long I had to wait to see him again.

# # # # #

Two weeks passed before I heard from or saw my Keeto again. As usual, our meeting took place on a late night. I had agreed to stay behind and lock up the diner, praying that he would find it in himself to have mercy on me and grace me with as little as his seductive smile. That would have been enough to hold me until the next encounter.

"Be careful walking home tonight!" Crystal warned. "That sick bastard is still out there, right in our neighborhood! They've found four more guys since last week."

Debra chimed in, "It's always guys, good looking guys, in your age bracket, Tesmond."

"Some sick, homo, psycho!" Crystal nodded. "Whoever the sick fuck is injects them with some weird substance. The paper says they haven't been able to figure out exactly what it is, but they figure it has to be what's killing them, 'cause they never find trauma to the bodies."

"I can take care of myself, ladies," I sighed, spraying the stoves down with oven cleaner.

If they expected me to be frightened by some maniac with a hypodermic needle, they had obviously forgotten all of my years of mixed martial arts training. Besides, I felt confident that

Keeto would show up to walk me home that night. I can't explain how I knew, but I seemed to feel him lingering near.

"You just be careful, pretty boy!" Debra begged. "I know you want to feel like a big man, and all of that, but I'm leaving this pepper spray on the counter. Take it when you leave."

"Do it for us!" Crystal added, sensing that I felt insulted by the mere idea of carrying some date-rape prevention tool.

"Ladies, it's only a few blocks! I've made the trip a thousand times before, and when I was a lot younger."

A sudden pounding on the door caused us to all jump around, wondering who had ignored the flashing, neon sign that signaled our closing.

"We're closed!" Debra motioned towards the sign. "Goddamn you, asshole; I said we're closed!"

The guy at the door continued to bang for a few seconds, and then headed in the opposite direction.

"Weirdo!" Crystal shook all over. "Will you walk us to the car, Tes?"

"And put my life in jeopardy?" I joked. "Come on, according to you, the killer only targets guys. Who would be safer out there, you or me?" I had been pulling my jacket on the whole while I talked, preparing to escort them across the parking lot, though I was sure it was needless. The guy at the door was probably just some drunken frat boy from the local college, too far in party mode to have deciphered the closed sign. It wouldn't have been the first time that happened.

"Be careful!" Crystal reminded as they drove off.

I waved them away with agitation and walked back towards the diner, fidgeting in my pocket to find the keys. Just when I was preparing to enter the building, the sound of footsteps caused me to whirl around. "Keeto?" I breathed, but was disappointed to find that it was only the asshole from before, the one who couldn't see the closed sign.

"Is there a phone in there I can use, bro?" he drunkenly drawled.

"No. Sorry. I can't let anyone in once we're closed. We've been closed for more than thirty minutes!" I chided, pointing to the flashing sign. "There's a payphone a few blocks down."

"Shit!" he groaned in defeat. "Can I at least follow you in long enough to take a piss?"

"Sorry!" I said more sternly. "I can't let anyone in once we've closed. We are closed; that means you can't come in, not even to piss!"

He gave me a challenging look, and when I didn't back down, he headed in the other direction, mumbling to himself about what an asshole I was as he tried to stay erect on his sloppy, drunk legs.

After watching him leave the premises, I double checked the trash to make sure Debra hadn't just thrown it in the barrel in her usual manner, leaving the bags exposed for every stray dog with a hungry belly and a good nose to stroll the contents all over the parking lot. I certainly didn't feel like cleaning it up the next morning, nor did I feel like catching the heat from her actions. I knew that my mom blamed me for everything that went wrong. I was supposed to have enough pride in the family business to double check behind every employee, though I got paid the least of any.

I was pleasantly surprised that I finally didn't have to re-do the job. Again, I prepared to enter the building, but this time, it was Keeto who stopped me. "Guess who?" he kidded, coming up behind me and covering my eyes with his hands. He kissed my neck, and I leaned my head back into his chest, wondering how the hell I hadn't heard his footsteps on the wet pavement. "Did you miss me?"

"Yes," I admitted, pulling free from his embrace. "It seems that's all I ever do, and I'm tired of it! I want some answers from you tonight, Keeto!"

"Okay," he swallowed, apparently caught off guard by my reaction. "Be careful what you ask me, though. I can't lie, and you may not be able to live with the truth."

I grew so agitated with his mystery man routine that I wanted to hit him. Instead, I rambled off a series of questions: "What does that mean? What is the truth? Why do you always disappear on me, Keeto? What is it that you're running from? I know you like me. Is there somebody else in your life?" I had already decided that if he couldn't give me straight up answers, this would be our last encounter.

"No," he promised. "There is nobody else in my life." His eyes saddened as he added, "I'm as alone now as I've always been."

"But you don't have to be alone. I want to be with you! That's all I ever think about. The only thing stopping that from happening is you and this disappearing bullshit that you always pull!"

"It's not that simple."

"But it is that simple!" I pleaded, wrapping my arms around him. "Keeto, I love you. I know I don't know you as well as I should before I say that, but I do. I know you love me, too,

108

whether you can admit it or not! I feel it when you hold me, when you kiss me, and I felt it the other day, when you did what the hell ever that was you did to me."

"That was a mistake," he shuttered. "You are right; I do love you, probably more than I have ever cared about anybody in a very long time. That is why I am going to beg you: please, don't love me!"

"What?" I asked, totally confused. When he held me, it didn't feel as if he was only interested in physical gratification. The way he stroked my skin, the way he kissed me, even the way he stared in my eyes and held my hand as we talked, told me that I meant more to him than just another sexual conquest. If that had been the case, why had he been content with letting me have all the pleasure on our last encounter?

"You have to promise me that you won't tell me that you love me again," he begged. "We can't love each other, and we can never make love, ever!"

"Bullshit! Why can't I love you? Why did you stop yourself from making love to me the other day when I begged you to? Is it AIDS, Keeto? If you're sick, we can be careful."

"Sickness is not a luxury extended to my kind," he sighed, stepping away as I attempted to kiss his lips.

"Then what is it?" I screamed, so angry that tears bounced down my flushed cheeks. The wind carried my echoing voice throughout the parking lot.

"To make love to me is suicide, Tesmond. You and I were never even meant to coexist on the same plain. There is no condom that can shield you from my poison."

"What the hell are you talking about?"

109

"Hell is exactly right," he shrugged. "I'm sure you've heard the story, how we fell from heaven." Despite my look, which questioned his sanity, he continued to talk, as if he were making all the sense in the world, as if he was unburdening himself with what he was disclosing. "I was weak and stupid back then: we all were, young and weak. We followed him because he promised us something better. Better than heaven; can you even imagine that?"

"Stop it with this crazy bullshit! Give me straight answers."

"I am! Tesmond, I lost my place in heaven because I listened to the promise of something more, something forbidden. I won't make that mistake twice. Looking in your eyes is the closest I've come to being home, and I won't lose my heaven a second time!" He stared at me with sincerity and stroked my cheek.

I couldn't help but release a hysterical laugh. "So, you got kicked out of heaven with Satan? You're telling me that you're a demon?" I couldn't tell if it was from the wind that had just started to pick up, or the threat of standing alone with someone so insane, but I began to tremble with chills.

"Those are your words. I said, 'angel,' fallen, but still an angel." He lit a cigarette.

"Assuming that I buy this shit for one moment, which, by the way, I totally don't, what has that got to do with you being with me? You've already fallen from God's graces; what more can happen to you?"

"It's not me that I worry about. Like I've told you, to make love to me is suicide for your kind. Don't you see that? This is my punishment ... my hell ... to never truly enjoy the one temptation that caused me to turn my back on God. Everyone I

110

make love to dies. That is why I can't love you, and why I won't make love to you. My first time with you will be your last. My punishment is never to enjoy the same lover twice."

"Okay, Keeto!" I laughed. "You win the craziest mother fucker award, hands down. If this is the best you can come up with, then I'm glad to say goodbye to you before I invest anymore of my time."

"Wait!" he begged as I attempted to enter the diner again. "I can prove it to you. Promise me that you won't breathe a word of what you see to anybody else, and I'll prove it."

"How will you do that? You going to show me your wings?" I joked. "Is that what you're hiding under this baggy shirt?"

"No." He pushed my hands away, and said, very matter of fact, "Those were taken from us when we were kicked out."

"Jesus, Keeto! You've made it clear to me that you don't want anything else to do with me. Why don't you just stop this crazy shit and leave me to the rest of my life? Enjoy the rest of yours, you crazy fuck!"

"I can prove it!" he begged. "Do you see that guy over there?"

"Yeah. So?" I shrugged, noticing the drunk from before staggering back towards us. "Is he going to vouch for you? Is he one of the fallen, too, one of your heavenly homies?"

"Hey, bro!" the sloppy drunk called to me as he approached. "If it's not asking too much, can I borrow some change? I got all the way to the fucking payphone and realized I had nada. My cunt girlfriend's mother won't accept a collect."

111

"Get the fuck out of here!" I exploded. "I don't give a fuck about you, or your girlfriend, or her cunt mother! I don't have any change, and if I did, you couldn't have it, just because I find you and the stench of your cheap liquor so fucking repulsive!"

"O-fucking-kay, asshole!" he screamed in my face. I prepared to deck him, but Keeto stepped between us. The drunken fucker turned to Keeto and said, "Bro, will you do me a solid, loan me some change?"

"You won't be needing it," Keeto smiled. He walked closer to him and ran his hands down his chest.

"What the fuck are you doing?" the asshole drawled. "Get your fagot hands off of me, mother fucker? I asked you for change, man, but that don't mean I want to hump you for it! I ought to kick your goddamn ass!"

"You will do no such thing!" Keeto smirked. He grabbed the sides of the drunk's head, and I watched as the sloppy bastard's body convulsed with a familiar pleasure. When he let him go, the poor specimen's legs wobbled under him, even more than before. His eyes widened, and he ran his own hands over his body signaling the burning passion within. I could see his hard cock straining against the leg of his denim shorts.

"What the fuck did you do to me?" he asked, seemingly, frightened, but equally aroused. "God, man, what was that?"

"Shhh!" Keeto warned, and pulled him close again. The pitiful drunk welcomed the embrace this time, roaming Keeto's body with lustful hands. Their lips met, and the guy began to tremble. I had no doubt that he would have crumpled to the ground had Keeto's strong arms not been wrapped around his waist, pulling his crotch into contact with his own.

"Oh, God!" he panted, wrapping his legs around Keeto's waist, just as I'd always felt the need to do whenever Keeto kissed me. "I don't know what you're doing to me, but don't you stop it! Don't you dare-fucking-stop!"

"I have no intention of stopping," Keeto purred, and spun the boy around so that I could catch a better glimpse of their entanglement. His hands savagely ripped through the fabric of the guy's tight underwear, which were already visible beneath the gaping waist of his sagging shorts. Two smooth, brown, hairless mounds tumbled free, flexing and jiggling as he gyrated against Keeto's torso, covering his neck and face with sloppy, drunken kisses. Keeto traced the divide in them with his fingers, and I grew stiff and jealous as I watched.

"Fuck me!" the drunk begged, letting one arm fall free from Keeto's neck long enough for his hand to reach between the two of them and squeeze Keeto's humongous bulge. "I want that in me right now!"

"As you wish," Keeto moaned and freed the biggest cock I had ever seen from his sweat pants. It had to be more than fifteen inches long, and it curved to the left. Every vein in it was illuminated by the flashing, neon sign of the diner. It appeared to be coated in some white, slimy substance, far too thick to be precum, and far too rich in color to be Vaseline or lubricant.

"UUUUMPH!" the giddy drunk moaned as the enormous head was positioned to stab inside of him. He shivered all over and fell against Keeto, limp as a rag doll, when it was shoved all the way in. He wrapped his arms tighter around Keeto to aid himself in bearing the pain, or was it pleasure? I couldn't decipher from his airy moans. "MMMMMM ... HMMMMM ... MMMMMMMPH!"

My mouth went dry as I watched the encounter. A huge lump of panic formed in the back of my throat, forbidding a scream from coming. Keeto stood completely still, his arms fastened around the boy's waist. His thighs, legs and hips also remained immobile and steadfast, but his cock pushed itself in and out of the boy's stretched hole. I had seen many pornos and, not even professional fuckers had managed that feat. It appeared that the cock had a life of its own, a faceless serpent, slithering in and out of the drunk boy's guts, and he seemed to enjoy every second of it. "Don't stop, you son of a bitch!" he begged Keeto. "Don't you ever-fucking- stop!"

Keeto repaid the boy's moans of delight with silence. His eyes remained focused on me, as I fumbled behind myself for the door knob. If I had only been able to make my legs move, I would have hauled ass into the diner and locked the door behind me, but as frightened as I was, I couldn't tear my eyes away from the grotesquely arousing sight.

Keeto's bottom lip remained tucked between his teeth, so there was no way he could have been talking to me, but I swear I heard his voice surround me. "Don't be afraid!" he pleaded. "I would never hurt you, not for anything in this world, nor for the promise of something greater."

The drunk appeared twice as turned on as I was frightened, and I was nearly scared to the point of pissing. He reached behind himself, spreading his cheeks for the beast of a cock to roam further inside of him, and gnashed his head from side to side in ecstasy. He repeatedly kissed Keeto's face, wanting another taste of the lips that had him more intoxicated than the cheap liquor that coursed through is body. When Keeto denied him that, he settled for sucking on his neck.

"Here it goes!" Keeto grunted, pulling the boy tighter to himself. "I'm going to shoot my poison out inside of you!"

"Every goddamn drop!" the ignorant drunk pleaded, seemingly oblivious to the fact that Keeto had just referred to his seed as poison. "Give me every fucking drop! Don't you let me go until you do! Don't you goddamn dare!"

Keeto's body shuttered violently, and he screamed so loudly that my ears popped. His mouth never opened, not even a hint, so I wondered if I had been imagining the sound, until the drunk freed his hands from Keeto's body long enough to shield his own ears from the perpetual, high pitched shriek. The streetlight flickered above us, and the glass globe shattered.

When the sound finally ended, the drunk was thrown to the ground, shaking as violently as Keeto had done. He tore at his clothes, freeing his own lust-weighted cock. Semen poured forth, more bountiful than I can describe, painting him and the sidewalk beneath him. His asshole opened and closed viciously. Something became visible inside of him, stretching his rippled stomach as it moved, slowly working its way upward in his torso. He groped at it with his hands, his eyes widening with fear and pain. "Get it out of me!" he screamed. "Goddamn it, what did you put in me?"

"It'll be over soon," Keeto promised, kneeling to hold the poor bastard's hands as he twitched and begged for mercy. He cradled the guy's head in his lap, and ran his fingers over his eyes, closing them as he hummed a tune that was so ethereal and soothing, too complex to be reproduced by a human. The boy stopped his clawing and squirming, and a smile came to his face as he stiffened, his head fell limp in Keeto's lap. I had no doubt that he was dead.

"Keeto, what are you?" I was finally able to fight through the panic to ask. "What the hell did you just do to him?"

"I've already told you," he smiled. His mouth still remained closed as he talked to me. "I think you believe me now, and you understand why you and I can't be together."

"Why then, Keeto? Why did you come to me in the first place?"

"Weakness." He finally opened his mouth. "I was lead to you by someone stronger than you can ever imagine. I don't know exactly why, but he wanted me to destroy you. What he didn't count on was me making use of the one gift that God didn't take from us when he kicked us out, free will."

"Why me?" I shuttered. "What do I have to do with any of this? I don't even believe in any of this stuff! I'm just some boy who works at his mother's diner to save cash for a car."

"He saw something in you that he didn't like, probably a sign of great things to come. I don't know exactly what yet, but I see that promise in you, too; that's why I couldn't go through with your destruction." He was talking to me with his mind again, his lips were loaned to the task of lapping semen from the dead drunk's body. The sight was repulsive and arousing at the same time.

"So, it was you ... who killed all the guys they've been finding around town?"

"You make it sound more brutal than it is." He stopped lapping at the fluids and stood long enough to talk to me in a normal manner. "I didn't kill anyone. I made love to them. To love me is to die; it is that simple. My time with them, though short, was the most alive they ever felt. I gave them more pleasure in that short time than the majority of your kind ever is privileged to know."

"I can't deal with this!" I trembled, doubling over to vomit. A dead body lay right behind my family's place of business, and I was talking to an angel, or demon, or whatever the technical term was. It was too much. "Just go, Keeto!" I begged.

"I understand," Keeto whispered, appearing behind me to wrap his arms around my trembling body.

"Stop touching me," I moaned, still weakened by his scent and soft caress. "I don't know how much longer I can resist the temptation."

"Don't worry. I'll be strong for both of us. After tonight, you will hear from me no more. Never breathe a word of this to anybody, but know that I will always be watching over you. When the rustling of the trees seems to call your name, that's me. When the wind seems to caress your face, that will be me."

"So, I guess this is goodbye ... forever, huh?"

"Only for a while," he promised. "I will watch over you all of your days. When you have lived a full, joyous life, I will return to you in your last moments. I will make love to you when you are on your sick bed, and my touch will relieve you of all your suffering." He kissed the back of my neck, and before I could whirl around and get one final taste of his lips, he was gone.

I walked home, took a shower, and tried to force myself to sleep, but rest wouldn't come easy. I thought about the dead drunk, possibly still lying outside my mother's diner. I thought about angels and demons, and heaven and hell, and everything else that I had written off as mythological until recently. I thought about what Keeto had said about me having some divine purpose in all of the nonsense. That part is probably what kept me up the most, along with the reality that I would never see my first true love again.

I began to cry so hard that my bed shook. That is when I felt the weight of somebody else in my bed. I felt strong arms wrap around me, and I smelled a familiar, but indescribable sweet musk. "Sleep," the intruder lulled into my ear, and with those words, my panic subsided. I was out like a light, dreaming about my first kiss with Keeto, the pleasure he had given me behind the dumpsters, and his promise to return to me in my old age. I dreamed of that moment, over and over, until morning came.

When I woke the next morning, the house was buzzing with panicked voices.

"This guy makes number twelve." Crystal reported. "And the cop said he thinks they can link this same sicko to the dead guys they're finding four cities away."

"No more talk about all this!" Mama shrieked. "That could have been my son!"

"The sick fuck went too far this time!" Uncle June fumed. "Right outside our place! The cops knocking at our door to ask us questions, like we're criminals. We got to have our source of income shut down for God knows how long, while they pick their noses and walk around in circles, asking dumb questions!"

Without even journeying downstairs, I knew that the poor drunk's body had been discovered behind our diner. I no longer had the luxury of telling myself that the previous night had all been a dream.

"Damn you, Keeto!" I thought aloud, climbing from the serenity of my bed. That is when I felt the chill of a summer's breeze rush in through my window, a window that I was always careful to never leave opened. I also hadn't been dreaming when I'd felt him behind me, drying my eyes and lulling me to sleep. I smiled as I thought back to his promise: When the wind seems to caress your face, that will be me. I smiled, and placed my hand over my cheek as the wind tickled my face. "I'm going to miss you, Keeto," I whispered before putting the window down.

OF CHOCOLATE AND METAPHORS
By Junior

I.

"Your mighty serpent crawled up inside me

And pierced my stomach with its probing head

Its body ever stretching, never recoiling

As it spewed its hot, white venom deep in my guts

Then slithered out of me

Leaving me with a deeper respect for snakes."

Treshawn Mann was relieved to hear applause after he finished reciting his poem at the Welmon College fall talent show. Treshawn's roommate, Demarques Shad, aka Chocolate, was grinning from ear to ear out in the audience.

Treshawn was especially glad that Demarques liked his poem. He wished he had the nerve to tell Demarques that the poem was inspired by a wet dream he'd had of him. Demarques was Treshawn's ultimate crush. Demarques was tall with an athletic build, rich dark, silky skin, soft wavy hair, and deep brown eyes. The icing on the perfect chocolate cake for

119

Treshawn was the fact that Demarques was also gay and wrote poetry.

Treshawn did not win the talent show, but seeing Demarques smiling and loving his poem made him feel as if he'd won the grand prize.

# # # # #

"Props and pounds, my nigga," said Demarques giving him a fist bump after everything was over. "That was brave and tight as hell; you should have won."

"Now you know a poem about me getting fucked up the ass wasn't going to beat out any of the gospel numbers, Chocolate."

"And man did they really start singing them when you finished," teased Demarques. Treshawn chuckled. Before he could come up with a funny response, Everette, Demarques's part time piece of ass swished over.

"Ooh Yello!" He screeched with girlish glee. "That poem was the shit."

"Thank you," said Treshawn, pissed by the fact that Everette, whom he practically grew up with, still called him Yello, the nick name he despised.

"No honey, thank you, cause I am in the mood to have a big assed snake crawling all up me; Chocolate, what you doing later?"

"Damn Everette! Have some tact," frowned Demarques.

"What the fuck ever tact is, believe me I'd rather have some dick instead; what you doing later, Chocolate?"

"Get the fuck away from me," hissed Demarques in disgust. "For real, Everette, go!"

"Fuck you, Chocolate." Everette rolled his eyes. "Your poem was fuck'n stupid," he hissed at Treshawn before stomping off.

"You sweet bitch!" Treshawn shouted behind Everette. He and Demarques burst into laughter.

"Hey, you fucked him," teased Treshawn

"Don't remind me."

"Seriously though, what are you doing later?"

"Oh, you want some dick?"

"Hell fuck'n yeah," thought Treshawn, but he laughed it off and said, "No crazy; I was wondering if you wanted go to the pizza shop and grab a slice or go hang out at the coffee house and listen to some of the poets."

"The coffee house sounds like what's up," said Demarques.

"I got one more class, and then we'll meet up around seven."

"Sounds good." They gave each other pounds then walked away in opposite directions, each of them regretting not having said more.

II.

Treshawn returned to his and Demarques's dorm room wearing only a towel. His slender frame still moist from the shower. Demarques looked up from his laptop and frowned.

"What's wrong?" asked Treshawn.

"I can't come up with the right metaphors. I got this kick ass poem in mind, but I can't find the metaphors."

"It isn't mandatory that a poem has metaphors ... or rhymes for that matter."

Treshawn removed his towel and with his back turned to Demarques began to apply lotion to his body. Demarques admired the master piece that was Treshawn's ass.

"Two golden cakes," said Demarques out loud

"Huh?"

"I found the perfect metaphor for your ass; two golden cakes, sweet and tempting, daring me just to nibble, when I'm longing to devour"

Treshawn did not see nor hear Demarques get up from the computer desk and walk across the floor. He felt Demarques embrace him from behind. Treshawn inhaled, deeply. Demarques still wore his boxer briefs, and Treshawn loved the way the material, stretched by Demarques' hard dick, felt against his own naked ass.

"I'm about to really give you an appreciation for snakes ..."

Treshawn woke suddenly, sitting upright in bed. His boxers were saturated in his discharge.

"You okay?" asked Demarques.

"Yea, I just need to wash up." Treshawn was embarrassed to get out of bed and let Demarques see the mess he'd made in his underwear, but going back to sleep with the wet sticky goop in his crotch and running down his thigh was out of the question.

"Goddamn, who were you dreaming about?"

"I don't even remember," lied Treshawn going over to the sink and removing his stained boxers. Like in his dream, Treshawn did not hear Demarques come up behind him.

"Chocolate!" he said startled as Demarques's firm hand took the wash cloth from him and proceeded to wash his dick, all the while grinding on his naked ass from behind. Like his dream, Treshawn loved the feel of Demarques's hard dick rubbing against his naked ass through boxer shorts. Demarques alternated between kissing Treshawn's neck and nibbling on his ear during the bathing.

Treshawn's penis had been thoroughly cleansed and aroused to the point of appearing purplish. Demarques turned him around so that the two of them were face to face. Demarques dropped to his knees and continued to stroke it with his hands. Treshawn could feel the warm moist lips approaching and knew that he was in for something wonderful. He was the most surprised to hear himself say, "Chocolate don't." just as Demarques was about to fully take him in his mouth.

"Okay," said Demarques getting up off his knees and heaving a heavy sigh of frustration.

"I just don't want things to get weird between us," apologized Treshawn.

"They already have," mumbled Demarques as he climbed back into bed and pulled the covers over his head.

III.

Two nights later, Treshawn woke to what he thought was an earth quake. The floor and his bed were shaking. The moans and groans coming from Demarques's bed were animalistic. In the dimness of Demarques's nightlight, Treshawn could see Everette riding Demarques with reckless abandon.

"Hey Goddamn it!" roared Treshawn as he sprang out of bed and hit the switch, flooding the room with light. Everette rode on.

"Excuse you," said Treshawn literally snatching Everette off on Demarques and hurling him to the floor. "I got a fuck'n early class; ya'll may have to meet up and do this shit some other time."

"Damn Treshawn! You didn't have to throw nobody," said Demarques. When Demarques got up off the bed to check on Everette who hadn't moved since being "placed" on the floor, Treshawn got the first look at his naked, semi hard dick. The total length and girth of it made Treshawn wonder how Everette's little narrow ass wasn't broken in half.

Demarques helped Everette get up and gather his clothes. As soon as Everette was out the door, he turned to Treshawn and raged, "That shit was foul, and you fuck'n know it!"

"What's foul is you two fucking all loud, while I'm trying to sleep."

"It never bothered you before, so what's really up."

"Kiss my ass, Chocolate, I was the one who said no to you."

"That's right; you did, so why did you block my nut tonight?"

"I'm done with it; like I said, I have an early class."

"Don't think I'm not gonna fuck when I want, too."
Demarques's words fell on deaf ears, as Treshawn had already
pulled the covers over his head.

IV.

"I hate that nigga so bad

I just want to cram my dick down his

throat and make him choke on all the shit he

talked to me. I want to bend him over

and mount him doggy style like the bitch he is

just ram rod him with no condom or lube

so he can feel the friction I have for his ass

I want to fuck the arrogance out of him and skeet

my frustration all down his back

Damn I love that nigga so bad

I just want to curl up in his arms

and feel safe

I want him to treasure me like a mother

treasures her newborn. I want my heart /my hands/

my mouth/my ass/my dick/ my balls to be his reasons for
breathing

conflicted in how I feel about this nigga

one minute wanna kill this nigga

the next wanna take my own life for this nigga

I'm conflicted

Man, Fuck that nigga!"

The coffee house patrons roared with applause when Treshawn finished reciting his poem. The recent friction with Demarques had made him quite prolific. He only wished Demarques could have heard the poem that he inspired. Treshawn sat at the counter and pondered for the umpteenth time in two weeks why he didn't fuck Demarques that night. He had wanted to do so since the first day he met him. The truth of the matter was that Treshawn was in love with Demarques, and he did not know if Demarques felt the same. He could be content with being fuck buddies with any other guy on campus, but he had to have more with Demarques. His thoughts were interrupted by a fine brown skinned brother with a low fade, wearing a pair of baggy jeans and an oversized black T-shirt. Treshawn immediately recognized that he was a member of the rap group that performed earlier. Their music left a lot to be desired for Treshawn. It was typical hyper masculine, hyper sexual, chauvinist trash that perpetuated stereotypes about black men. Fucking bitches and getting high was the theme of every song.

"What's up? My name is Romey; I liked your poem."

"Thanks, Romey; your group was good," lied Treshawn

"So, you into that homo shit, huh?"

Disgusted, Treshawn was about to leave when Romey grabbed his arm. "Wait man, I ain't tripping." Romey looked around to see if anyone was listening before saying. "I gets down like that, too; I got a girl and all, but sometimes a brother's gotta scratch the itch."

"You seem cool, Romey, but I really gotta go before the dorm closes."

"Let me walk you back to campus."

Treshawn never said yes or no; he just headed for the door, and Romey followed.

Treshawn was grateful that the walk back to campus was only ten minutes. He could not endure another second of Romey discussing the size of his dick and how long it had been since he'd gotten freaky with another dude. Treshawn said goodnight at the lobby entrance, but Romey followed him to his room.

"Romey, I really gotta go to bed; I got an exam in the morning."

"Why you tripping?" asked Romey. "You know damn well I want to fuck!"

"That is not my problem; now please leave before I call security." Romey walked away. Treshawn made the mistake of not making sure he was gone before turning his back and opening his room door. Without warning, he was seized from behind and forced into the room. Treshawn fell to the floor with Romey on top of his back. In the dim light, he could see that Demarques was in bed, "Oh God, Chocolate, please wake up."

Treshawn tried to struggle, but Romey's thick muscular build was too much for his slim frame to fend off. Treshawn tried to call out for Demarques, but Romey had a choke hold on him.

"I'm gonna teach your yellow ass about teasing my fuck'n dick." Romey ripped at Treshawn's cargo pants all the while proclaiming in graphic details how he intended to fuck him right there on the floor.

When Demarques opened his eyes, it took a second for him to piece together what was going on. The image he saw in the dim light did not look like a consensual ordeal. He was certain that Treshawn wasn't the fuck on the floor type. He bolted out of bed and pounced on Romey who had damn near completely disrobed Treshawn. Demarques locked Romey in a tight head lock. Treshawn scampered to his feet and turned the lights on.

"I will snap your fuck'n neck!" he warned. "Treshawn open the door." Treshawn did as he was told. "You fuck with him again, and I will murder your ass." Demarques shoved Romey into the hallway and slammed the door behind him.

"Did he hurt you?" he asked a visibly shaken Treshawn.

"I'll be ok," said Treshawn.

"You're shaking; come here." Demarques wrapped his arms around Treshawn and guided him over to his bed. "You're cold as ice," he proclaimed, wrapping him and Treshawn up in his navy blue blanket.

"He followed me; I told him to get lost but ..." Treshawn's sobs cut off the rest of the sentence. Demarques wrapped his arms around him tighter.

V.

Treshawn woke up alone in Demarques's bed. Demarques held him all through the night, but they didn't do it. Treshawn respected Demarques for not taking advantage of him when he was vulnerable. The previous night assured him that Demarques was the one for him.

Treshawn's cell phone buzzed just as he got out of bed. The message from Demarques requested that Treshawn meet him at Lonnie's apartment around nine. Lonnie, the owner of the off campus party house was cool with Demarques. Treshawn figured the Lonnie was throwing another of his infamous Friday bashes and Demarques wanted him to come and have a good time after what had happened last night. Treshawn figured that a party was better than feeling sorry for himself. He decided that after he and Demarques returned from the party, he would let Demarques know how he felt about him. He was certain that Demarques felt the same way about him. Both of them just needed to quit with the stunts and shows and tell the other what was really up. Treshawn would take the initiative.

VI.

There were no cars or bikes parked outside of Lonnie's. No music shook the sidewalk, and there were no people running about outside, drunk and high out their minds. "Am I too early?" Treshawn wondered. Nervously, he knocked on the door. Demarques opened it, and Treshawn felt himself go weak in the knees. Demarques wore a white fitted cashmere sweater that accentuated his fabulous physique and made his dark skin appear even more smooth and inviting. His white fitted jeans showed off his impressive bulge without being vulgar. Treshawn struggled to restrain himself from behaving as Romey had the night before. He'd always thought that Demarques was sexy, but damn, the brother had him hot and horny.

"Looks like I'm early for the party," smiled Treshawn as he entered Lonnie apartment.

"No, you're right on time for our party"

Treshawn noticed for the first time the dimmed lights and the abundance of black love scented candles throughout the living room, down the hall, and glowing in the bedroom beyond. Demarques guided him over to Lonnie's purple suede couch. "Make yourself comfortable; I've got something I want to share with you," said Demarques as he stood in the center of the living room floor. "This poem came to me last night when I was holding you, Treshawn, and I wanted things to be special when I read it, so I asked Lonnie to let me use the crib while he's away for the weekend." Demarques took a couple of deep breaths to ease the nervous tension he was filling before he began.

"I thought I liked Dark colas best

But now a Mello–Yello's got me feinding

And like lemonade on a hot summer's day

You're all that I am needing

I want put your straw inside my mouth

And taste your sweet libation

I wanna drink you down /all the way down

To the bottom of the glass

Sip you slow, never fast

Cause I want to prolong this liquid sensation

Hold the ice

I want you straight

So fizzy nice

I just can't wait

I wanna swallow you down

And let you tickle my insides

The way the butterflies often do

Whenever I start to think about

130

How much I want a drink of you"

Treshawn was so hard it hurt at the thought of Demarques's beautiful lips sucking him off. Rather than speak or applaud, he stood before Demarques and removed every stitch of clothing he had on. Demarques, following Treshawn's lead, did the same. Demarques dropped to his knees right there in the living room, and took Treshawn's ample cock in his mouth. Treshawn wanted to kick his own ass for not allowing Demarques to service him weeks ago. Treshawn held tightly to the back of Demarques's head and fucked his mouth with the same intensity he hoped Demarques would later fuck his ass. The thought of having Demarques's big black dick deep inside his ass made Treshawn erupt. Demarques swallowed every drop, fulfilling his desire to drink Treshawn down. Demarques lifted Treshawn and placed him on Lonnie's computer desk. If the dick sucking hadn't been treat enough, Demarques ate Treshawn' ass causing the pretty pink puckered hole to glisten like an exotic flower damp with dew. "Goddamn, you taste so good," exclaimed Demarques. "I could do this forever, but I gotta get up in them guts; you gonna let me touch that stomach baby?"

"Yes," panted Treshawn, eager for Demarques to fuck him. He leaned forward and sucked on Demarques's monster for a few minutes making sure to get it extra wet. When he was ready, Demarques climbed up on the table on top of Treshawn and lifted his legs above his shoulder. Demarques pounded away like a man possessed. Treshawn's screaming and moaning and the possibility of the desk breaking beneath them only motivated him to go faster, deeper, harder.

"Oh God! Chocolate, you're in my stomach!" screeched Treshawn. "You're in my stomach!"

"That's where I wanna be," panted Demarques, steady pumping. He could feel his climax building. "I love you so damn much boy!" he exploded right inside of Treshawn, filling his hole up with warm, milky cream of nature.

"Love you, too," panted Treshawn as Demarques fell spent against him.

VII.

Treshawn and Demarques did manage to make it to the bedroom by the third time they fucked that night. The third time they both agreed would be the last until the soreness wore off for both of them.

Demarques held Treshawn tight in his arms as he had the night before.

"Thank you," said Demarques

"For what?" asked Treshawn

"For letting me help you gain a deeper respect for snakes."

Treshawn kissed him on the lips. "Thank you."

"For what?" smiled Demarques

"Metaphors."

They nestled closer together, two men content, and drifted to sleep in each other's arms.

THAT THING
By Rawiya

Hard to believe that I'd have so much to do this morning, but it's a Monday after all. Of course, because of last night's events with my latest lover, I didn't want to get out of bed at all.

"Fuck ..." I mouthed to myself. My feet touched the cold floor while I ran my fingers through my long hair. The new man in my life thinks it's cute. So instead of my prior idea to cut it, I've decided to keep it, so he would be able to run his fingers through the curls.

And oh, did he.

I really should've asked him to stay over ...

Then again, he couldn't. He does have a wife and kids to go home to. Nevertheless, he let me know that this thing, as he calls it, was so good. The man couldn't bring himself around to saying that he might be gay, but it's alright, I'm sure he'll eventually come around.

But when? How long will it take?

Will the urge to leave his spouse be something quick or will it take longer like say, a few months or years till I turned thirty? God, I hoped not.

When would he say goodbye to straight life and hello to that big rainbow colored door?

I know it'll be hard for him, discarding the so called normal existence for the one that's damned to hell. Where everyone criticizes and hates you for being different. The one, where besides the color of your skin, you're just as likely to be shunned by your peers, discriminated against, not treated with high value, but I think I'm worth it, aren't I?

Aren't I, Sergeant Lawrence Bernard?

# # # # #

Going into a club where most of the patrons are straight, you don't expect too much action. However, since my best gal pal, Dania, insisted on taking me out that night, I refused to be around a bunch of queens anyhow. It had only been a week since I'd broken it off with my latest jerk, Antonio. I'd caught him screwing around with some woman in my bed, after coming home from another writers' gathering. Not something I wanted to see, especially since they were fucking on my three hundred count sheets.

"C'mon, Jamison … let's dance." She pulled me out to the dance floor, and like a lost puppy, I followed. We held hands, trying to keep the rhythm, when I spotted a hot man sitting at the bar, staring in our direction.

I tapped Dania on the shoulder, putting my mouth close to her ear. "Hey babes, go talk with the nice one, gawking at you. I'll be over here, drinking my sorrows away."

She looked around, as did I. Just as I was about to depart, she pulled my hand. "He isn't looking at me, dumbass. He's checkin' you out."

I rolled my eyes, sighing, "No way. That man is as straight as they come." We kept moving out the way of the other people.

"I just found out while he was glancing this way. He shook his head no. He pointed in your direction. Go talk to him."

"Uh uh, noo ..." I waved my hands frantically. We were yelling at each other over the blaring music. Not paying attention, we didn't bother to check the bar again for our voyeur. Before we knew it, I felt a hand on my back.

I whipped around, looking at our mystery man, in the eye. "Hi," I said loudly. I felt Dania touch me before she left.

"Hey, how about a dance?" He held out his hand. "Lawrence Bernard."

I raised an eyebrow, putting my palm inside his. "Jamison Sterling."

Once we started moving, nothing more was said until five songs later when he took me back to his spot at the bar, buying me a drink. We sat right next to each other, trying to hold a conversation even with all the noise. We did pretty good, until another song I liked came on. I led him to the floor, dancing closely to him, not even wondering about his situation. The bottom line was, he was hot, and I wanted someone to pay attention to me other than Dania.

There was no substitute for male companionship, especially for a gay man, even when you are on the mend.

# # # # #

I walked to my bathroom, turning on the showerhead before stepping in front of the medicine cabinet mirror. Immediately, the thoughts of my man came to mind. His caramel skin against my pale white flesh. We looked lovely together. A beautiful black man and a handsome white one. Yin and yang we may be, but still a lovely combination.

Dreaming, I closed my eyes, recalling the night before, when his big, strong, arms were around me. My hand reached to rub the top of his bald head, while his hardened muscle was at my puckered entry. We stood there, drying each other off after enjoying a hot bubble bath.

"Jami ... tonight's the night, right?" He called me Jami, short for Jamison.

I looked at his wild brown eyes through the glass. "Yes, I told you I was ready to give it up."

Once he kissed the side of my face, I shifted around to face him. "Lawrence, are you sure you want this? I know you're worried about what people will think."

Lawrence placed a small peck on my lips. "I'm not gonna lie to you, I am, but ... I'm gonna have to come to grips with it sooner or later. We been seeing each other for damn near six months."

"Well," I interrupted wrapping my arms around his waist, "You're the one that has the charmed life and reputation. As long as you say you want it, I'll be here to help you get over your fears."

Lawrence grinned, "That's what I like about you, Jami. You've been patient with me; you don't bullshit me either. Just for that, I would say you'd be worth all the crap that's gonna come my way."

I chuckled, "I'm glad to hear that, Lawrence. Now ..." I dragged my fingers down his slender torso, gripping his tight buttocks, while giving him a small kiss on his mouth. Right then, his lips engulfed mine, his tongue wrestling, pinning it down.

"Show me baby ... show me that I'm worth it."

Lawrence flashed that wicked smile that attracted me to him months ago in Roundabout. "You know I will."

No words were spoken after that. Promptly, he picked me up, carrying me to my bedroom, laying me on the mattress. His head dipped between my legs while pushing them apart, so we could enjoy our first time making love. Yep, it would be our initial try since I'd let my honorably discharged officer know there would be no sex until I was sure he was ready to accept this thing, and although he still had trouble saying it, I'd let it go because it wasn't the easiest decision to become a scrutinized member of society, especially when you've spent your whole life being celebrated.

"Fuck yes …" I closed my eyes tightly as his mouth began to work on my cock, tasting the precum that formed on my swollen head. "Damn, what have you been watching?"

Lawrence laughed, "Some video on the net when the house is asleep. I need to show you some new tricks I learned."

"Unnmmhmmm …" I moaned, caressing his shaved scalp as he made a trail with his tongue down to my perineum. "Ohhhh … shiiittt …" The pleasure was overtaking me. All I could think about was …

# # # # #

RING RING

"Sometimes you got me …"

"Damn …" I was startled by a ringtone of one of my favorite dance tunes. The one I picked for my man, something that signified our relationship. I walked quickly over to my nightstand, grabbing the phone. "Well hello, you callin' me to say you're changin' your mind about this thing," I chuckled. I'd heard it before, so it would be nothing new.

The voice on the other end cackled. "No … that's why I like you, Jami. You're so fuckin' sarcastic."

I plopped on my bed, my morning wood hitting my stomach. "I have to be after all the shitty ass relationships I've had. Aren't you supposed to be playin' good man and father right now?"

"She's gone. She took the kids to her mom's house … and since I was alone, I was wonderin'…"

"What?" I raised an eyebrow while looking at my nails. "I have a lot of things to do today, my friend. If you're talkin' gettin' together, maybe later …" I had to keep him off balance. I didn't want him to think I was already craving for him, even though I was.

"C'mon baby … I can imagine you may be busy but."

I rolled my eyes. "Such is the life of being self employed. Not all of us were given money by the government or married to a woman who's a millionaire."

Lawrence's laugh came through a little loud, making me pull the phone away from my ear. "Babe, please, she'll be gone all day. When we made love last night …"

"We didn't make love, hun. It was just a good ol' fashioned fuck. The first time in a man's ass will getcha' every time." I smirked, waiting for his response.

Again, a loud roar. "Damn you kill me. Don't make me beg for it; I know you want this as much as I do."

I turned up my top lip, sighing, pondering: did I have time to fit my new man into my busy schedule. I had promised myself that I'd never do this, especially with men who were still on the fence, but deep down, there was no question I wanted his chocolate dipping into my milky cup once again. Right now, that was so much more appealing then taking things to the cleaners, going to the bank to make a mortgage payment, or more importantly, getting the final edits done for my next novel that my editor had asked for about three weeks ago. "Um, well, alright, if you must, you must, but you gotta be outta here by three. I have things I need to do."

"Yeah right, once I get there, you'll change your mind, I'll see you in a bit, baby." I heard the loud smooch through the phone and then the recorded message.

"Fuck." I yelled, tossing my Blackberry onto the bed. "I promised myself I wouldn't."

And I did, of course, because the man was just so damn delicious. It was easy to change my mind about the errands. Having sex over things to do was always a no-brainer.

The door to my heart, which I swore I would keep closed, was being unlocked. Although it excited me to have someone in my life again, it scared the shit out of me because he wasn't sure of what he wanted.

While getting all wrapped up in someone, I'd lost out so many times to the other man or the unsuspecting woman in his relationship, that it hardened me, and made this twenty-six-year-old think twice about getting in too deep but damn, I couldn't help it, sometimes rules were just meant to be broken. "Sucker. It's that damn look on his face, well toned, body ... fuck me ..."

I never said I had a lot of will power ...

Now that my days plans had been changed, I might as well get some rest until my Lawrence comes knocking on my door. I will need it since the tender side of fucking will take him some time to master. Although, I loved a little roughness, I don't really enjoy the after effects of being manhandled like a sack of potatoes.

Just something else we needed to work on …

I lay my head on the pillow, pulling the covers over me, thinking about my officer again; retired by thirty, U.S. Navy man, discharged because of an injury that occurred while fighting the senseless battles in Iraq. He was so happy to be out of the war zone. Did he know he'd be entering another being with me?

# # # # #

"Fuck …" he yelled loudly as his cock pried me open. What can I say, it had been a while.

"Yesss …" I bit my lip as he began to pound me into submission, his hard flesh hitting mine was a rhythmic sound, almost like a drum beat.

Lawrence leaned over me, "God, you feel so good …" He kissed me, wrapping my legs around his waist.

"Uh huh, really? Better than your older wife?"

Lawrence laughed. "You certainly do, Jamison. Besides, I didn't marry for the love anyhow; I did it because she was willing to put a seventeen-year-old poor black kid through college."

"And then you joined the armed forces to get away from her." I completed that sentence, and he pushed into me harder. "Umph."

"Yep, you would, too, if you had to force yourself to love someone that you had no feelings for. Gettin' hitched to an old woman was the best decision ever for a closeted man. Fuckin' would only take a few minutes, and after that, she'd be asleep."

I laughed, "Yeah? Well damn, she must be in the minority because I have a lot of forty plus female friends who have the libido of women half their age. If I didn't know any better, it sounds as if you were with a woman old enough to be your grandma."

"Nope, just one that had a lot going on when she was young. Damn." He threw back his head. "God, what have I been denying all my life."

"Something that feels amazing. Do it faster baby, ride me, already." I placed my hands on his shoulders, shoving upwards into his groin. "Fuck me, Lawrence, don't hold back."

Once I said that, he obeyed, thrusting into my not so tight space, making it ache. "Shit, yessss …"

"Oh my GOODDDD." He called out, leaning over me again, engulfing my lips. Lawrence's tongue tangled with mine, sampling the tastes of Starbucks latte, nicotine, and Merlot.

"Sh … iii … baby …" He released my mouth. The sounds of skin slapping along with our moans filled the air. "Ohh yesss … God."

That moment, I felt Lawrence's latex expanding inside of me. Quickly, he pulled out, spurting his juices on my pale flesh. I ran my index finger through his natural juices, putting a little into my mouth. I watched him tremble while his hand continued to jerk his own man meat. "Ohh damn, Jamison …" His chest was rising and collapsing, the tattoos on his abs glistening with sweat.

"Shit ..." I mouthed, encasing my shaft with my moist hand. "Damn, what a beautiful sight."

Lawrence laughed, "Your turn, baby, c'mon, I wanna drink you."

"But you already did, you want some more?" I moistened my lips while handling my own cock. My groin wanted to explode, gawking into his light eyes.

"Fuck you're so hot ... I won't be able to resist you."

"Ohhhh ..." the jizz began to ooze out of the slit. Immediately, my man's head was between my thighs, gulping down everything I had to offer. His fingers sliding in and out of my puckered hole, making me gasp. I bit my lip. "Goddd ... Lawrrrrreeennncccee ..."

"Mmm ..." he moaned while lapping up every drop. He left a little on the side of his mouth for me to taste while we kissed. When we stopped, he gazed into my chocolate orbs. "Damn ... this thing ... it's so fuckin' good."

I ran my hand over his wet forehead. "Yes that's right, it's just another kind of love is all, the best and one that's worth fighting for."

# # # # #

I lay in my bed, smiling in a not so deep slumber when I heard the doorbell.

It's him

I dragged myself out, walking slowly towards the door in nothing but my boxer briefs. My hard-on was painful at this moment, but I knew I'd be getting a release. I looked through the peephole at my man with a gleam in his eye. I opened the door.

"Well hello," I smiled. Before I could say another word, his arms were wrapped around me, lifting me from the hardwood floor. His lips enveloped mine. His tongue forced its way inside my mouth. "Damn baby, I guess you are happy to see me."

"Mhmm," he groaned, putting me back down. "I missed you so much. And since you said we only fucked last night, I wanted to take the day to make love to you." He leaned against my door till it closed. Lawrence reeled me in. The moment our bodies crashed into one another, I was ready to drop my underwear. He buried his head into my neck, biting lightly on my flesh while gripping my hips through the tight material.

"Fuck, Lawwwreenccee." I yelled. My arms rested on his shoulders. "God yes."

"You want this, don't you?" He rubbed his crotch against mine. "Uhhmmm."

My breath caught as he picked me up again, this time carrying me to my sofa. He dropped me there, discarding his clothes, piece by piece, while staring at me.

Such a lovely sight he was. I wondered if this thing, as he called it, would be the best thing that's ever happened to me.

FOOT LONG JOHNSON
By R. Talent

I nearly creamed in my boxers the first time I saw him. Not only did the man look delectably sweet, but also he smelled extremely good, leaving me with a whiff of his cologne as he passed me by in the narrow hallway.

Although he had been living right next door to me for at least the last six months, I never saw him before that day. All I knew of him was that he lived with his girlfriend who had a tendency to let everyone on our floor know when he was a complete and utter ass. She did this by spouting off her latest suspicions of his "alleged" infidelity, armed with so much proof that she had me rooting for her to throw his then-faceless sorry ass out on the street. Some days, she had the jury convinced that she would, letting everybody know that she wasn't one of those ordinary pieces of cunt that would just put up with anything just to keep a man. The way she said it – so harshly in her raw native Caribbean accent – she sometimes had me on edge thinking that she was just a voodoo spell away from turning him into a chicken or something weird like that. She came close a few times, really close, saying stuff that I couldn't really make any sense of. But then he always managed to do or say something that often left her speaking in tongues for about an hour or so to the backdrop of a very squeaky bed for the same amount of time. Sometimes it felt like the best fuck of our lives, as I sometimes found myself propped up against my pillows playing with my wet asshole and proudly dripping dick to their vigorous lovemaking through the thin walls.

As I finally put a face to the man that forever forced my hand into buying a dildo, I prayed that I wasn't too obvious in my staring as I was unhurried to unlock the door to my apartment. He was such a handsome soul. Just to say that he was good-looking was simply an understatement. He was far beyond that. And to call him gorgeous wasn't going to suffice either. With his smooth clean-shaven face, the ultimate tragedy was that he was fully aware of his good-looks, knowing that his alluring smugness could make knees buckle all around him. Not only were his looks striking, but he also had noticeable height on him accompanied by muscles that just hugged his clothes. And to leave it at just that was also an understatement in and of itself, too. He was a tower of strapping muscles that the gods chose to dust in a permanent coat of fine cocoa powder, standing massive at six-foot-five and two hundred and something or other pounds.

I lingered around out in the hallway a few minutes more before going inside. I wanted to hold on to the exact place I was standing when I first saw such perfection, but not before I saw his girlfriend come out of her apartment with a favorable smile on her face.

It was one of those good days apparently.

# # # # #

"Give Daddy some of that pussy, girl! Give Daddy all that sweet pussy! It's mine for the taking, huh?! It's mine for the taking, huh, now, bitch?!? That's what I thought! That's what I thought! Yeah, bitch!"

"Oh Gawd, yes," the bitch screamed breathlessly in West Indies dialect to the rhythmic beat of the squeaking bed.

"Yes, what, ho? Whose pussy is this for the taking?"

"It's yours for the taking, Dad-d-d-d-y! Yours for the motherfucking taking! Take my pussy, Dad-d-d-d-y! Ohhh, take my pussy!

"AarrrghhhhHH!"

Precisely two weeks after I laid eyes on such a beautiful man out in the hallway, his presence still lingered with me down to the last detail as his handsome face came clearly into mind as his growls of passion came roaring through the wall. It probably wouldn't have been so shameful if I wasn't buck-naked onto top of Oscar thoroughly pumping in and out of my well-lubed asshole almost every night – twice whenever the nameless man over there was doing due diligence in fucking his girl. Oscar was my substitute man for the moment, someone who came in real handy during my extreme drought. He was always dependable, and frankly didn't give a shit whose face I put on him. Then, of course, he also wasn't real. He was nothing more than my well-crafted, chocolate-covered realistic dildo with a suction base cup that I mounted onto an old telephone book that I chose to ride out on top of my bed. While Oscar might not have had any beef with me fantasizing about the straight boy next door, I surely did. I had too many porn stars from my collection and on the web to choose from to even begin torturing myself like that. Even though my headspace was on the right track, the seat of my pants was the one in the driver's seat, with the most generous amount of lube mixed in with my natural ass juices running out of me to drench the penetrable beast as I continuously thought about him over there.

"That's it, give Big Daddy this pussy!"

Even though I was no virgin, I quickly found out that I wasn't exactly a whore either, as I tried earnestly to take the full length of the nine-inch insertable. On a good day, I was able to take about six or seven inches with no problem. But it nearly felt like my asshole was being ripped open trying to go down that extra mile to rock bottom. Yet, that didn't stop me from trying to slide further down the imaginary cock of my real-life daddy over there.

"It's your pussy Daddy! Take your sweet pussy!" She screamed like a wounded animal with the sounds of her sopping cunt even beginning to come through the walls as well.

After I left my girlfriend some time back, I had no use for pussy anymore. But the way he kept her satisfied every night made me slightly jealous, envious even, that she could be so free to be with him like that in the same spirit that my asshole craved to be free with a throbbing dick inside of it.

"Keep those pussy juices splashing back on this big dick, bitch! Yeahhhh!"

I could hear her pussy juices slurping louder and louder with an ear-deafening pop that suggested that he was excavating to her bottom of her lungs. The excitement of the two had my asshole convulsing with some of the clearest fluids to ever soak the telephone book and the sheets beneath me. I was more than ready to drain my balls of its tormented load, but I knew he was quite close to busting his own nutt. And after he had brought me this far in vicarious pleasure, it felt like some sort of betrayal if I came first, especially since in months past I could almost pinpoint the millisecond he came.

I couldn't hold off much longer even though he was close to coming over there. Oscar was thoroughly abusing my prostate, causing my head to spin in this sexual frenzy as I kept steady with the ferocious pace over there.

"Open wide bitch, me and my dick coming for that nasty snatch!" The nameless bastard grunted, and he came and came hard.

148

I tried to hold off for a few seconds more, but his rumble from next door was just too much. I was shaking and vibrating and I shot my nutt all across the bed. As it was all coming out of me, I began sliding further down Oscar with no brakes, getting down on him further than I ever had before. It was then and only then that I realized that I had everything Oscar had to give me plugged up my butt. I tried to get off of him, but my legs were cramped. My thick muscular thighs folded on top of them.

It was while I was trying to get my legs out of their locked position that I heard the telephone ring over there. I thought nothing of it at first. He was telling her to simply ignore the incoming call. Her argument was that it could be something important. Whatever it was, a deafening silence soon ensued followed by an incessant crescendo of screaming and shouting by his girlfriend that just blasted through the thin walls like a bass. It went from one end of the apartment to the other with her shrieking for him to get the hell out! Next thing I know I hear the front door slam shut with him out in the hallway. I made it to the front of my apartment just in time to hear him mumble something out there. I just couldn't exactly make out what he was trying to say. But I distinctly heard him when he put his fist to the wall out there because it shook my pictures on the front wall.

"Oh my God," I said stressing out each syllable, daring to look out of my peephole to the constant stomping outside of my door. There he was, pacing furiously up and down the hallway in nothing more than a pair of black briefs that looked to me more like a wide-band thong. If I thought his body was incredible with clothes on, I was getting wet and open all over again looking at his incredible body without them. His big bare feet supporting his well-sculpted calves and chiseled thighs were just mere compliments to the cobblestone of abs and the series of cryptic tattoos that covered his broad chest and bulky arms.

I looked through the peephole at him shooting in and out of eyesight a few times before he simply disappeared from view.

I had just come to the conclusion that he decided to stay committed to the other end of the hallway and try to talk to his girl again. I turned away for barely one second and when I got my eye focused out of the peephole, he scared the shit out of me looking back at me with the upper part of his face distorted.

"Oh shit," I mumbled louder than I expected. Giving some sort of confirmation that he was standing on the other side of my door. I held my breath not wanting him to know that I had been watching him. But I was too afraid to step away without making a noise to let him know that I was just that close to the door.

Then my raggedy doorbell rang. And before I could make a move, he rang it again, called out for anybody being at home before knocking on the door.

Because I was still buck-naked, I stepped away from my door and ran into my bedroom to throw on a pair of briefs that I left on the floor.

"Who is it?" I shouted as I pulled them up.

"You're neighbor from next door."

"Yeah," I said moving back towards my front door. "What do you want?"

"My girl and I live next door to you, and I got locked out of my apartment."

"What you want me to do about it?" I asked, trying my best to sound green to their argument.

"I was hoping that I could come in and make a phone call, talk her into letting me back in."

"How do I know you're telling the truth? I don't know anybody on this floor like that." I added to reinforce that we weren't such good neighbors for me to just extend a helping hand like that.

"Man, forget it!" He barked, throwing up his hand as I overplayed mine.

As I watched him move disappointedly out of the eyesight of the peephole in the other direction, I decided to slowly open my front door and wave him on in.

"What did you do?" I asked, closing the door behind him and noticing that the peephole too failed to do him any justice with these two hard fleshly globes coming together to form the world's most perfect ass. If I was a bolder and much more shameless man, I would've just reached out and touched!

"Man, that evil bitch is tripping!" He shouted, snapping me back into the moment. "She's on her period or something! She thinks that just because my ex-bitch is still in stalker mode that I'm still fucking that ho!"

"Damn," I mumbled.

Had the circumstance been normal, it probably would've been a cute way to express to him openly about what I thought of him as I passed it off as a clever response to what he was saying. But at that particular moment, my phrase was geared towards the slight funky whiff of my clean but recently open asshole running up my nose. It wasn't a bad scent as it was vaguely noticeable to me as I hoped that I was the only one who got wind of it.

I barely had a second to question my insecurities when I cringed at him taking a seat on my couch in front of my coffee table. I was cursing myself every step of the way for not doing a quick inspection of my apartment before letting this stranger in.

As a grown man living on my own, with no family in the region, my home is my domain as well as a place where I bring my pieces back. So, in kind, it is decorated with an erotic aura that is meant to be a conversation piece amongst good friends and arousing for those that are just simply passing through on their way to my bedroom. On my coffee table was a blatant display of half-naked black and brown men along with a poster from Tony Butcher's *Studies in Black* series, featuring a well-endowed naked black man with a white sheet over his head in the corner that I knew he couldn't have missed. Don't get me wrong; I have absolutely no shame in being gay as much as I wasn't in the mood to feel as if I had to prove my manhood to some heterosexual stranger. I mean, Yeah, I got down. Yeah, I like get my asshole pumped! But not once had I ever forgot that I also carried a dick between my legs or the baritone in my voice.

"You must've done something terrible for her to put you out in your drawers?" I said, hoping to take his attention away from my coffee table.

"No. Tracee is like that pop song, she's hot and she's cold, sometimes. She was in pure heat about five minutes ago, but after she got her fill of the stick, she went back to being the royal Ice Queen pain in the ass I know her to be."

"She got her fill of what?" I asked, aiming for him to repeat that part of his answer.

"The stick," he said bluntly. "You know the d-i-c-k," he emphasized even further by moving his thick hand over towards the soft noticeable bulge. "Judging by these books you should know what it is quite well."

He laughed. And it wasn't one of those sexy laughs that left me with butterflies in my stomach. It was one of those hard, hearty laughs that dashed any hope that he even played for my team much less gave gay men like me any respect as a man.

"Hey, there's no shame in my game. At least I didn't get tossed out in my underwear by some woman." I snapped, listening to his laughter soften.

"You just like walking around in your apartment in yours, huh?" He snickered, trying to break some the remaining tension, as he reminded me that I was playing in dangerous territory. That I was just like a hormone-driven teenager, just a hair away from sprouting a full-on erection without much encouragement. "I didn't mean anything by it, man. It's just that it sounded like you wanted me to explain what I meant what I said when you got the proof in those books right there."

"I don't need any proof in those books, partner. All I got to do is look straight down to see for myself." I offered matter-of-factly.

"I feel you. But, like I said, I honestly didn't mean anything by it. I'm just not myself after that bitch put me out in only this. I was wondering if I could make a couple of phone calls. I was thinking that if I can't get her to get right tonight maybe I can hit up one of my boys to let me crash with them for tonight – at least until this blows over."

"Sounds like a decent plan." I said, walking over to the breakfast bar that separated my kitchen from my living room to retrieve my phone.

He had a shouting match with his girlfriend and neither one of his boys, whose number he knew by heart, were at home, so he left a pleading messages for them to call him back on my phone.

I stayed behind the counter, in my kitchen, of course, once again self-conscious that my dick was willing to tell him how I really felt about him – in spite of his arrogance, of course.

And being behind the counter gave me the freedom to admire his incredible body.

"Want something to drink?" I graciously asked, looking at him with his head in his hands pondering his next move.

"Yeah," he smiled. "What do you got?"

I rattled of to him a number of choices, ranging from water to soft drinks to some alcoholic beverages that I had chilling in the refrigerator especially reserved for company like him. He was reluctant to accept anything at first. But then he decided to take me up on an offer of a glass of water before changing his mind and asking for the soft drink before lastly changing his mind again in wanting some liquor, but only with the request that I join him in a bottle.

We knew where his mind was. He saw that it was getting late, and if nobody called him back, he was going to be hung out to dry. Obviously, I wasn't going to put him out with nowhere to go. But being that he knew I was gay now, he figured that he could work me over for a place to stay for the night. And because he knew better than to just offer me sex, he thought he could get me tipsy enough for me to offer him a loose-lip invitation for him to spend the night. Preferably with no sex involved.

As much as I wanted to get mad at the sad little game that he thought he was running on me, I couldn't. I've been where he's been too many times to remember, with both guys and girls, to suddenly turn my nose up at him, learning the raw lesson that sometimes closed legs don't get fed. Back then, of course, I was slightly younger and still playing the field on the down low, hopping the bus to catch up with a late-night creep.

After we downed our fourth round of the rum-laced concoctions, I came to the brilliant conclusion that I was right and wrong about him. I was right about him trying to get me tipsy, but totally wrong about his motive. I can't exactly pinpoint what gave him away as much as I can say that after it was revealed to me what it was that I concluded that he wasn't above getting down and messing around. In fact, the way his eyes glossed over, looking dead at me, he was genuinely hoping for it. And with the two of us being drunk and horny and in our underwear didn't help matters either, with bulges growing and dying right before our eyes.

After awhile it was starting to play out like one of those bad pornos where we both already knew we were about to have sex, but we were forced to give useless dialogue for the unknown audience in desperate need of a storyline. As I was trying to find a way to cast aside preconceived notions about us not having sex, he just came out of nowhere and started attacking my face with these sensual kisses. Maybe my senses were heightened by the alcohol. Maybe I was just sexually frustrated from my six-month drought. Whatever it was, I was lost in this sea of tongue and lips feverishly caressing my face and neck.

Because of the alcohol, it took me a moment to get that I wasn't spinning upside down. But rather, I was on my back on the sofa with the armrest supporting the back of my head enjoying this magnificent god grinding on top of me. As his body was calling for my touch, I couldn't find the will to move my hands away from his head, rubbing it as if was a wishing lantern or something just as exotic. I was too busy not noticing that I wasn't groping his muscles that I was unaware that his hands were roaming my body until he started to pull my briefs off of me.

"Wait," I mouthed, but I really didn't want him to stop.

One might think that getting ready to fuck a guy whose faithful girlfriend was right on the other side of that thin wall might have stopped me, but no. My thoughts weren't even on her. My distinct thought in that moment was that he was too good-looking of a guy to have everything going for him. By everything, I was thinking of the size of his dick. I would be foolish to rationalize a drunken state of mind, but I would be lying if I said that it wasn't in the forefront of my mind. Even though I saw the bulge and knew he had stamina, the way Oscar ripped me open like he did, I wasn't worrying about not taking it from this guy as I was about not feeling it when he took it.

He had pulled my briefs over my ankles and feet before he stood up and took off his briefs as well. What I saw next astounded me. Now, before I go any further, I'm not one of those guys that get crazy about a big dick because even throughout all of my whoring around I never became that skilled of a bottom. But when I say that a size queen would have frothed at the mouth at the size of anaconda dangling between his legs, I'm not lying! I quickly had to sober up after seeing that, cringing at the thought that he wanted to put ALL of that up in me. Oscar damn near tore me an extended asshole, and this guy had the mythical foot long Johnson and wanted to ensure that I never walked straight again!

I mean if his dick was some random man on street, it certainly would be a ruthless motherfucker that simply did wrong shit just for the hell of it. And it was ready to go to battle with my tender butt hole.

"I see you like what you see," he said, moving back and forth letting the long sleeping giant sway between his thighs. "Why don't you work your way down to your knees and give it a closer look."

I froze. While I was still afraid of what possible harm it could do to me, I was also mildly curious, given the fact that I spent a great amount of time fantasizing about this man in the time passed.

He must have been the snake charmer or something because I have absolutely no recollection of how I got from off of the couch to kneeling in front of his awe-inspiring dick. But I did notice that it still had her juices on there, or rather her vaguely fishy-feminine scent.

"I know you want to taste my dick after I finished fucking my bitch over there, right? Taste all of her on every inch of me … all in your mouth! Finishing up where she started off."

I wanted to put in my mouth on it, but greatly feared being that guy. You know that guy – that guy that will do just about anything for a piece of dick. Then I realized that this was going to be a give and take. I was going to give him a place to stay for the night, and I was going to take his dick to the head for a sizeable deposit.

I took the head of his enormous dick cautiously passed my teeth and slid it over my tongue. He moaned in pleasure, which only encouraged me to foolishly take more of him into my mouth. Not only was he good-looking black man packing a long dick, but also he was enormously thick, like two-handed lead pipe-thick. I tried to get wild with it, turned on by the euphoria of it all, reaching through his wide-stance legs to get two handfuls of his hard, sexy butt, pushing him into me. But I guess he reasonably took that to mean that I was very skilled in taking on magnum men his size. He had me held down by the hook of my head choking and gurgling against the never-ending feast of meat filling my mouth. And yet, I still tried to be accommodating to him, relaxing my mouth with short circular strokes of sweet-tasting pre-nutt painting the back of my small throat.

"Lick my balls, boy," he commanded in a calm tone. It wasn't like he was trying to be dominating as he was going for being firm. "I want them vibrating in your mouth."

I hummed against his balls, still tasting her on him

"When was the last time a real man got to that ass?"

157

"Huh?" I asked pulling my face out of his crotch. I heard him quite well, but I was still breathless from gulping down his stiff shaft and overcoming the aromatic intoxication of his man-scent invading my nostrils.

He repeated the question still, and I gave him some obscure answer that he didn't pay much mind to. I was still melancholy that the last time I had sex with another man was the day before my beloved boyfriend chose to have a threesome with two of my so-called closest friends while I was at work building our future together.

"I'm not worried about your last dude." He offered. "As long as that hole can put a grip on this dick, I'm good!"

"It'll grip," I said, wrestling with my ultimate decision to let him try and fuck me.

I sucked him off for a few minutes more, bringing him so close to the edge that we were about to rule out fucking altogether, but we stopped short of that marker. After I had his dick soaking with spit, he had his tongue drilling my ass. I probably would've been reluctant for such a treat, given how I was still greased up from earlier, except that I used the pineapple lube on my ass rather than the regular stuff, which drove his taste buds crazy.

I was just getting used to my legs being rolled over my head when he let my ass fall to his waist. I was expecting him to tease the hole just a bit more, giving me the mental resolve to finally go through with it, when he again let my ass fall to his waist and slid his dick up in me like it was nothing.

Although the spit and the lube were forgiving in letting him roam my guts like that, my insides felt like they were on fire.

"Take it out of me!" I cried in a pain I never experienced before.

He just looked at me and laughed, knowing for certain that this time he most definitely had the upper hand as he rolled my body to the front of the couch where he had more room to execute his most baneful plan.

"Relax that hole like you relaxed your throat, sweet boy," he said licking his full lips, trying to be assuring, leaning forward and steadily pushing his inches into me.

I wanted to tell the bastard to fuck off. Get it out of me! I wasn't even able to relax my throat because I was too deathly intimidated of all the thick remaining inches of dick that were unable to reach my lips. But sensing that he wasn't going stop just because I wanted him to, I had to do exactly what he said. Either that or have the untimely death by a killer dick.

"There you go. Give Daddy that sweet boy-pussy," he groaned movingly, stretching me out to limits I couldn't even believe I could be stretched.

I always hated it when guys call ass pussy, but I figured if that was what needed to get him off quick, fast, and in a hurry, I was game.

The way he was grunting through my screaming to get it further inside of me, I was damn near certain that he was just seconds away from losing his load right then and there. But the only one who lost it was me when I felt this tight grip in my rectum suddenly give way like a tight rope to a heavy load, letting his dick skewer my body like jelly.

"Oh, Gawd," were the words that simply escaped from my dry trembling mouth, not knowing if I was going to survive this uncalled for assault.

It was only after he got it down to the hilt twice, keeping the head of his dick inside of me when he retreated back, did the burning in my hole begin to subside. It never went away really, as this heated pleasure simply dwarfed it with him burying his massive snake down to the balls with his pubes playfully tickling the outside of my newly stretched-out hypersensitive hole.

"Oh, man, you're giving Big Daddy some of that tight sweet boy-pussy, aren't you? Aren't you?!" He moaned in confirmation with my kneecaps somewhere under my armpits just to receive him.

"Yes, Big Daddy," I mumbled with the breath knocked out of me, letting his face find my neck again. "It's yours to take! It's yours to take, motherfucker! Oh, Gawd, yes, take it!"

I only thought he was in the throws of fucking me before, but in fact he was just getting started. I didn't really understand the difference until he was ramming that anaconda of his into me as if my sole purpose in life was to lay there and joyfully take it.

And I did. He filled me like no other with the surreal sensation that I was getting my ass reamed by this cushioned piston. I bit down on my lip, feeling my dick stir with cum needing to be release with every forceful stroke he delivered to my prostate. He had me arching my back to relieve some of the tension, but it only turned me on more with his savage fucking, with his hand wrapped steady around my neck. He wasn't choking me as he was using it as a tool to keep me steadily in place. It was scary and hot at the same time, knowing that if got caught up in pounding out my hole that his grip could get a little tighter.

"Bang my hole, motherfucker! Bang my hole, you sexy-ass motherfucker!"

"I got you," he said in a sinister fashion.

Remembering the tempo he kept up when he was next door, I couldn't help but fear that I was about to experience the same hyper drive fate. Instead, he took to slow-stroking me, which proved to be more intense than his other rhythm. My body just reacted, with my hole just hungrily pulling his dick deeper into me.

"Oh, goddamn," I moaned with body tremors surging from my supersensitive colon through my body as a new urgency took over his. "Damn you!"

He didn't go back to the rhythm he had per se, but it was nonetheless intense, pulling his dick all the way out and pushing it all the way back in, proving to me that he had my hole stretched wide open.

"Where you want me to put it?" He asked, snapping me back to my senses.

"Flooded out, baby boy," I screamed. "Flood it out! Ohh!"

"Yeah, Big Daddy got you covered," he groaned with his voice coming out of his gut with his sweaty hands clenching my body before I felt his humungous dick swell even more followed by this stuttering war cry that filled the apartment. "I'M GOING TO NUTT OFF IN THIS BITCH! GIVE ME THAT SWEET PUSSY, BOY!"

# # # # #

I was still filled with his sloshing load the morning after when I realize that not only did I let this handsome stranger ruin my snug hole and did so without a rubber, but I also never got his name in the whole time we were together. But whenever I catch him out in the hallway in his drawers, he always leaves me with a smile on my face.

THE AUDUBON RULE
By Dandy Dixon

It was almost 2000. Y2k made palms sweaty. Nader made sense, especially at Victoryville University. There was a lot of hype on campus, not over the Green Party, but a party of rainbows at the student union. It was National Coming Out Day.

The next morning, on the cover of their school paper, a sophomore named Marshall had come out under a headline, which simply read "Loud and proud." A student body comprised mostly of chubby white people must have seen this admission, by the athletic and masculine young black male, as an item more newsworthy than the cafeteria workers' union battle, which was on page two.

Marshall made his announcement alongside some other queers, most notably, his friend Audubon. They inspired each other to come out at the same time and pledged to have each other's back for a lifetime. They were both just nineteen, but Audubon was lanky and decoratively femme (prompting a few "no duh" reactions about his surprise outing, but only under the breaths of passersby). When Audubon danced, the word "gazelle" buzzed like hot neon. He could don drag nearly nude; his pear-shaped curvatures made straight boys howl a little, before clearing their throats.

The other great thing about these two: even though Audubon was clearly the extrovert and Marshall, his thoughtful confidant, sexually it was a bizarre set of opposites. While the flamboyant Audubon preferred a quiet night cuddling under the covers, Marshall was easily bored by that concept. He often dreamed of massive orgy scenes, featuring all types of men, in the middle of the street, in broad daylight.

They were instantly drawn together, since orientation the year prior. A mutual attraction peppered the air around them, but their kinship formed such a strong bond, both young men were afraid to break it. Nonetheless, no topics were too taboo, and they enjoyed supporting each other's activities and passions. However, as the students urged others to step out of the shadows by coming out, a new tension began to build between them. They weren't in a relationship, and yet, there was still common wife-and-husbandry afoot, and they could communicate with each other without saying a word at those moments.

"Guess I'll never be the first black president now," said Marshall, holding up the front-page photo.

"Oh, please! As big a freak you are, you couldn't even be the first black manager of a Taco Bell."

Audubon was trying to pinpoint what it was, exactly, about Marshall that irritated him, but he couldn't put together any ideas that weren't hurtful. Marshall knew something had to be bothering his typically fabulous and carefree companion, so he invited him for a drink at Vito's.

Vito's was a straight bar, and a hole in the wall at that, but it was the only place around that didn't hassle them about being underage. Of course, there were a handful of gay bars even in an industrial town like Victoryville, but they seemed only to make their allowances for white boys. This reminder put a particular sting behind Audubon's question ...

"So what's up with you being a snow queen?"

Technically, Marshall wasn't a snow queen. Though his sheltered, bourgeoisie upbringing, and All-American prowess in lacrosse made him stand out in a crowd of African-American males, he never said he exclusively wanted white guys. No, Marshall just didn't believe he was attracted to other black men. You could very well be darker than he – from the darkest corners of exotic India – but if you were a black man, you didn't have a chance of ever hooking up with this bright, good-looking brother.

"I'm not a snow queen," Marshall was already pissed.

"Don't act like you ain't never seen a fine-ass brother before."

"Look, we can shut this conversation down right now. There's nothing wrong with having preferences."

"Right, like when I go online and some bitch is like 'White/Asian/Latin/Middle Eastern/Mediterranean/Mixed OK' and the whole time I'm thinking to myself, 'This bitch done picked every Crayon except mine!'"

"I'm not like that. I'm straight up horny. I don't discriminate, Bonnie."

"Whatever, Marsha! You ain't never said two words to me about even looking at a black man."

"Seriously? What am I supposed to do now, only bust my nuts on the West End?"

"All I'm saying is we share a lot of stories with each other; and yesterday we did the coming out thing, and to me that means you are letting it all be known."

"And I never would've done that without you. Audubon, you are my guardian angel. You know if I had some sort of issue I'd talk to you all about it."

"So why not us?"

"Hm?"

"I mean ... why not black people?"

Marshall didn't have an answer. He shrugged his shoulders and sunk into his pint of stout. He wanted to let his friend know that maybe he was onto something, but his pride stood in the way. It made him feel like he was being judged for a crime he hadn't committed. The pint went down much quicker than anticipated, and he decided to retreat, rather than refill.

"I wasn't trying to get you upset about anything," Audubon lied.

"It's cool. If you hear about a blizzard in tonight's forecast, it's probably just me, the snow queen. Peace."

Leaving Vito's in haste, Marshall had no intention of heading back to the dorms. In the crisp October night, the dirty Marshall was ready to bone the drama away. Perhaps the impulse was a little self-destructive, ready at the first sign of discomfort to fuck a smile back onto his face, if he has to.

I'll do whomever I want, whenever I want. That queenie bitch can't tell me shit, Marshall thought to himself. He searched through some business cards in the pouch of his backpack and came across Wesley's number. He was forty-one, a big white bear, with salt-and-peppered fur all over, including his soft bush surrounding a very thick, uncut cock.

They'd met coincidentally while uptown, buying weed from the same dude. First it was just eye contact, and on the way out the door the bear reached out and grabbed Marshall's sweet bubble ass. Wesley mentioned right away that he had been in a relationship with another man for about a dozen years and only acted with the approval of his beloved. Marshall saw no problem with this sort of occasional hook up because with every other guy, he was the one doing the topping.

Wesley could serve two purposes for Marshall this night. He wanted to get fucked, hard. And feeling Wesley's thick meat slide down his hole would also be the "so there" moment he could brag about later on (as in, Audubon's so hard-up he wishes he had hot white cock, or any cock, in his ass tonight so there.)

Although he was in a formally open relationship, Wesley had to take his play elsewhere. Marshall wasn't quite ready to sign him in and bring him up to his double either, where his death metal roommate, Zo, could come in at any moment. Zo was cool and all, but not that cool. So they agreed to meet at a cruising spot by the Riverwalk.

Without saying hello, Wesley turned Marshall around and bent him over a rail overlooking the water. Jeans came down, and the beefy man started pigging out on Marshall's hole. His full beard felt good in the young man's crack and back of his balls. What started as licks and sloppy kisses soon became a penetrating tongue fuck that sent Marshall's eyes toward the back of his head. Wesley used his large, strong hands to spread the juicy cheeks open and get deeper. Marshall started to make his butt bounce a little, up and down. The hairy bear must have enjoyed the view of the smooth, round and brown bootie jiggling as it rode his face, because he released guttural moans Audubon could feel vibrating up his ass.

Wesley unzipped and pulled his beer can dick out. Marshall got down on his knees and sucked on the hairy nut sack while helping put a condom on the rock hard meat. These nuts were huge, and felt so good in his mouth that he didn't want to stop, but Wesley was eager to get that black ass bouncing again. Marshall resumed his position over the railing. Wesley squirted a packet of lube on the hole and stuffed his short, yet thick cock inside.

The music of ass cheeks clapping off of thick thighs and the scale of pleasurable notes in Marshall's moans, were heard by lots of other cruisers on the marshland stretch. A handful of men gathered around, encouraging Wesley to slap it, squeeze it, spit on it, pound it, and grind it up. Marshall loved all the attention. Putting on such a submissive exhibition only got him hotter.

It only lasted about fifteen minutes, but it seemed like a marathon – especially when Wesley told him to get down on his knees and stick out his tongue. All the men took a few steps closer, tightening a ring around Marshall, who had begun stroking his wonderful nine-inch chocolate bar. One of his fantasies required all the different types of guys he was into spray him. What a night for that to happen!

The first one, from a young Chinese guy in a business suit, oozed onto his left cheek. The next shot, from a well-built Latino in his thirties, went up his nose, all over his tongue and down his chin. A couple of minutes later, the last two cruisers, both older white guys who were always out here, came on Marshall at once, and he was caught in the crossfire of daddy dick juice covering his eyelids and forehead. Wesley saved his fireworks for last, a milky bolt, followed by gobs and gobs pumped onto his sticky face. This college boy just took a bukkake icing those cruisers hadn't even seen in porn.

A few cheered and applauded Wesley's mighty load. One of the old men posed next to Marshall and took a picture of the creamy aftermath. Marshall loved being a pure slut like this. He finally stroked out a rope that covered one of Wesley's shoes in jizz.

It was the type of bizarre bonding moment men need more of. They were hugging each other and remarking on how beautiful Marshall was. The business suit guy gave him a bunch of napkins to wipe his face off, while the athletic Latin squirter left him his phone number and whispered in Marshall's ear that he was hotter than his wife. They congratulated Wesley on finding such a well-behaved, delicious young boyfriend, and he corrected them, saying his husband was at home.

Wesley was dominant, but gentle with Marshall. He walked him back to his dormitory from the cruising spot, holding hands, rubbing his bootie, and kissing his neck along the way. Once they arrived at the building, he said he wanted Marshall to spend an intimate evening with him and his partner in the near future. Without having to think twice, Marshall agreed. They kissed passionately as some student onlookers gawked a little.

A few days later, Marshall and Audubon sat next to each other in their weekly course on ethics in literature. Their very pregnant professor, Dr. Day, was the only African-American, male or female, with tenure at the university, so they automatically loved her. That's just how it worked. They wanted her to succeed, and would often compare the feeling of being in one of her classes to rooting for black characters on an '80s show, just because they were black.

She was leading a discussion about the story of *Billy Budd*. Marshall hadn't read the book, and had no idea what was going on. He tried to be smooth about glancing for a clue in Audubon's notes, and instead he was greeted with a disclaimer that read: "I KNOW YOU'RE READING THIS."

What else could Marshall do at this point besides continue to read? It said, "You're my boy, no matter what, but remember: before there was 'I'm Queer and I'm Proud,' there was 'I'm Black and I'm Proud!"

They looked at each other and smiled. Marshall figured it was best to keep communicating via notebook, responding, "But I need to make sure my flavor tastes like more than just 'Sup wit it? Wuz good my nigga?'"

Questions and answers were being raised all around them, but their silent conversation was twice as interesting. Audubon replied, "Just because a brother is a little street don't mean he ain't read *Billy Budd*, which is more than I can say for your sorry ass!"

"You're right," Marshall responded, "What do I know? But there are a few things I just might not be ready for yet."

"Do tell."

"Well, one thing is people, my people, are all just doing the same thing now. I don't want a guy saggin' and do-raggin' because that's so played out to me. Need somebody who wears grown-up clothes in the new millennium."

"Hell we only got til 2012 anyway!"

"Stop! You know that shit freaks me out! Just let me have my dirty dozen, and then the apocalypse can do what it wants to. Anyway – you talk about me shutting other folks out – but people turn on me, too."

"What do you mean?"

"They judge me. They tell me I'm trying to be white, or trying not to be black, and I don't know what else to say to these motherfuckers besides kiss my black ass."

"Keep saying that! It ain't about the status quo. You know a real black man when you see one."

"I hear you. There's just one more thing. You know, I think it has something to do with feeling a little too close to home. Like if you and I hooked up, I would literally be hooking up with my brother. You just remind me of my friends and my family – the people I really care for."

"That's a sweet thing to say ... everybody in your family ugly though."

They were chuckling uncontrollably at that point.

Professor Day suddenly jumped in, "Gentlemen, what are your thoughts in regards to the ethical dilemma Melville is attempting to illustrate?"

"People, please," Audubon always began his thoughts with a peculiar way of fine-tuning the nervous attention of everyone around him, and Marshall dearly admired this skill.

"Billy Budd wasn't on some thug shit," the slender queen continued. "He was just trying to knock the hater out and ended up killing him by mistake. He ain't some sort of talk show host. He can't just talk out his problems, like silly what's-her-face in the back is trying to say. He was just an average man, who spoke with his fists because the punk deserved a beatdown."

Everybody else in the class, white people, were stunned, but the professor held the sides of her eight-month belly as she laughed out loud for a moment. Then she moved on to silly what's-her-face in the back's raised hand.

He glanced over at Marshall's notebook, which read, "At first I thought I heard you say, 'negro please'."

Audubon had to go to another class immediately following this one, so they made plans to get together for a late night smokeout. What could put those plans in jeopardy? Once Marshall got back to his room, Zo let him know a guy named Wesley had just left a message. He knew what he had to do.

Wesley and his husband lived in the nearly gentrified Cherokee District of Victoryville. Wesley answered the door and told Marshall his husband was on the way home. Marshall hadn't really asked many questions about Wesley's partner before, just assuming it would be another hot and nasty bear who was probably a bottom. The apartment was surprisingly spacious and tall. The spines on good fiction decorated their walls, with shelves built from the floor to the ceiling. Everything seemed stylish and proper. Marshall thought this place was so clean he'd be afraid to touch anything – until he saw where things got dirty.

They had a playroom, which also doubled as his husband's office. A sling hung prominently in the center. A rim chair sat beside it. An assortment of plugs and dildos hung from the wall, meticulously displayed the way a samurai's weapons collection might. Brazilian bareback porn was being projected onto a screen. There were trays filled with poppers, lube, nipple enlargers and clamps, cock rings, etc.

Wesley lay down on the floor and slid under the rim chair. That was Marshall's cue. He got naked and squatted into the bottomless seat. This time, he got deep penetration with his tongue right away. The hairy bear reached every corner of the honey pot and licked it clean. He would suck Marshall's saggy pair of salty balls during intervals when he needed to catch his breath, but spent a significant amount of time sucking and tongue-fucking the tight black rosebud.

Then they made their way to the sling, and Marshall got in.

"Give it to me raw," Marshall said.

"OK, baby, but I'm not going to come inside you," replied Wesley.

"Why not?"

"Because I like watching my milk splash all over your tight little caramel body."

The hairy bear used a lube shooter to squirt oil deep into Marshall's ass and followed it, without hesitation with a balls deep cock stuffing. He kept his fat white dick in his ass while he reached for a blindfold.

"We don't want you to know the kinky things we're going to do to you tonight. We just want you to feel it," Wesley said.

After he tied on the blindfold and confirmed Marshall couldn't see anything, he took a snakebite kit and applied the little suction cups to Marshall's nipples. He then proceeded to pound him, the chains on the sling rattling louder with each thrust.

As the pumping got wetter and more intense, Wesley pulled his cock out of his ass, adjusted the sling's height slightly, and while Marshall's head was tilted back, he slapped him in the face with his dick. Marshall opened his jaw wide and could feel Wesley begin fucking his face even harder and deeper than he had been fucking his ass.

"Honey, I'm home," Marshall could hear someone who had entered the room say.

His voice was deep and soothing and warm. He could hear them kissing for a moment before the voice of Wesley's husband declared, "You were right about this one, Pickle. This is a hot fucking boy!"

"He's all ready for you," Wesley said. Though Marshall was in such a vulnerable position already, he didn't know what his fuck buddy meant until he started to feel the new dick in his ass and noticed right away that it was much larger than Wesley's (who certainly wasn't doing bad for himself in that category). While it was semi-hard, it was already the longest and heaviest piece of man meat that had ever been inside of him.

"Deep and wet like a hot fucking pussy," the unknown man said as he grabbed Marshall's ass and manipulated the sling like a machine, using a small fraction of his strength to propel Marshall's entire frame, suspended at the perfect height for face fucking and ass pounding all at once, onto a dick that Marshall was dying to see.

Whoa, God, Marshall was thinking, *this is a monster cock!*

Wesley finally took the suction cups off, leaving Marshall with swollen nips resembling giant Hershey Kisses. The fit college athlete felt one, then two pairs of lips feverishly suckling and nibbling his tits, and they felt more sensitive than the hair on his balls. If his tits could come, they would have popped like volcanoes, but instead he was helpless, shuddering and shaking as the sensations from his perky nipples rippled throughout his body.

Then the married couple kissed again, and soon Marshall could hear sloppy slurping sounds beside him.

"You wish you could watch my man deep throat my dong, don't you, boy? Suck it down, Wes. Suck that dick down your fucking throat the way I need it done, honey. Damn that's so fucking good."

Marshall could hear Wesley gagging on the monster cock, sucking more, and gagging again. As soon as Marshall wondered how Wesley was holding up, doing so much choking on such a big dick, he got to experience it firsthand. This time the major dong got to fuck his throat while Wesley shot some more lube into Marshall's hole and slid back inside.

They had him like a seesaw. As he went up, the husband held his head back and as big balls rubbed against his brow, he used his cock to tap into a deep throat Marshall didn't know he had until now. When he came down he was slamming onto Wesley's beefy bear cock. They had Marshall right where they each wanted him. For Wesley, the excitement took him by surprise as he took a step back and unloaded a yard of spunk that left a cum creek from one of Marshall's sweet cocoa nips, across his body, and down to his belly button.

"Take him down and let him watch me bang that butt," Wesley's partner instructed. They told Marshall to get down face down and ass up on the floor. Wesley slid a mirror into his husband's view as he mounted Marshall from behind. When Wesley finally took off his blindfold, Marshall found himself in front of a mirror, in a doggy position, and behind him was a very large, muscular, sexy black man who was also Wesley's age. He started slapping his dick on Marshall's ass so that he could confirm that it was indeed nearly a foot long.

"I'm Greg," he spoke into Marshall's ear while going deep and slow inside. Like Wesley, he was strong and assertive, but still kept a soft and sensitive tone. "Now let me wear that butt pussy out," he continued.

Marshall could now see his own ass jiggling as it bounced off of Greg's tree trunk thighs. His dark chocolate dick was breaking Marshall down upon each stroke. He thought he couldn't keep from screaming any longer, but it came out as a siren song of moans and delicate wails. Right there in front of him, he could see a big black cock taking control of his hole, and he loved it. He kept pumping it doggy and the party kept going. Another half hour had passed, and Marshall's buttocks became loose and wild, the ass-quake gyrated out of control as Greg masterfully directed every dip inside.

"Goddamn that bubble bootie is sucking the cum out of my motherfucking dick, honey," Greg at last confessed to Wesley. "This little brother takes my dong stroke for stroke, man!

Oh man! I can't believe you could take all my meat for so long you goddamn beautiful boy. Oh, shit baby ..."

And with that, Greg pulled out just in time. His blast overshot Marshall entirely and hit the mirror in front of them. But this married couple was ready to go again in no time. They knew Marshall hadn't unleashed his squirt yet, so they offered to help him out with that.

"No thanks," he told the hot couple. "But is it cool if I take a shower real quick?" They provided, and upon leaving he pledged to see them again. All night long next time.

Back at the dorms, he zipped directly to Audubon's room. He let himself in and saw his friend was sitting at his desk, putting the finishing touches on a cone-shaped joint. They hugged, as they typically did to greet each other, and Audubon noticed something else was greeting him as well.

"Ummm ... You know your penis just jumped up and poked me in the stomach, right?"

"Bonnie, I see the light," Marshall said.

"What?" Audubon had to sit down.

Marshall stood directly in front of him, so he couldn't help but lick his lips. Then he gently pulled his sweatpants down, revealing the hung shaft and low-swinging scrotum still filled with an impossible load of jizz. Audubon took it lovingly into his mouth. Once he had wrapped his lips around the base of Marshall's shaft, it felt for both of them like it was right where it belonged. Audubon sucked down that delicious dick as Marshall held his friend's hand and permitted him to take it down to the balls.

He held Audubon's hand tighter, squeezing Hail Mary's into it as the load rumbled in both of his fragile nuts. Such slippery head was sending Marshall over the top. Audubon's lips and tongue knew how to milk massage big dicks. He sucked it patiently, carefully, yet with purpose. When Marshall couldn't hold his best friend's hand any tighter he poured a warm bucket of cream in Audubon's mouth, who looked up into his man's eyes as he swallowed it.

They caught their breaths and lit the joint. Each one was a little unsure about what had just happened. They were only certain that they needed to do more of that. They took turns funneling smoke through a dryer sheet blow-tube, so generic spring fresh scents were in the air. Once it was time to ash it, they tightly embraced each other. From one friend to another, one thing that had always been uncertain for the both of them was no longer: they knew for sure that if they could come out together, they could do anything.

LOLLIPOP
By R. Talent

"C'mon, now, Clay, lick it up like a lollipop."

Even in my head-swimming hunger-pang daze, I knew the gritty baritone voice laughing right above me very well. For as long as I breathe air, I will never forget or forgive that monstrous voice. That voice I once mistook for soothing friendship just to lead me down the path of ruins, to be plugged by so many countless dicks in my sweet mouth and loosened asshole that nobody around my old neighborhood would ever let me live that shit down.

Thinking back on it, it started out so stupidly. I was so afraid of ever being called a lame by the bootylicious girls from around the way that I foolishly did everything in my power to become one. My first misstep was joining a gang that specialized in smash-and-grab robberies of high-end clothing stores. I had a good run before I got caught with some of the tags hanging out. After that, I was in and out of juvenile for the same thing so much that the system was one big turnstile for me. But when I became of age, and was looking for some kind of mentor, I got hooked on No-Good Rasool. I was young and in love and with no real guide into this "other" world; I was quickly coerced out of my pants by this older, smooth-talking player from around the way. And just when I got use to the idea of him roaming my guts with his powerful screwdriver, he sent me packing into confusion.

Though I got off on what we did, I refused to go out like some punk, forced to wear high heels and makeup like some flaming fag in heat. So one day, I caught a glimpse of myself in the mirror with my marijuana-flavored lollipop hanging between my lips and decided that I was one fine-looking motherfucker, with my slim frame and big swaying dick. I quickly found out that a lot of other people agreed with that assessment, too. Especially the way they threw them dollars at me while I gyrated naked in front of them. Soon, porn came knocking. I was being featured in these flicks with four other big dick black dudes jamming the same homely little white girl. It was enough to pay the bills but not enough to get what I wanted when I needed it, considering it was my face that was being branded for all eternity forcing some trailer trash cunt to lick up her ass juices off of my dick.

I guess somebody must've caught a ride on my wavelength because not long after that I got this call from this go-between that represent a bunch small dick white boys that got off on that shit, watching their girls become major cumdumps for some big black meat. I was pleasantly surprised when the go-between hooked me up with a few of my old running buddies, in particular Carlos, one of the older boys from my old neighborhood that I found myself jonesing for after I got turned out by Rasool. So when I caught a glimpse of what he was working with, I was fascinated. Especially the way that white girl hollered as he pummeled eleven-inches of his python-thick uncut meat inside of her.

Outside of the hired fucking, I came to discover that the short afro-wearing, stocky-built black man that I grew up with was quite talented as an artist, making some decent pocket change sketch white girls with cum dripping out of their mouths and cunt left there by their black lovers for their husbands and boyfriends to see on this cuckold website. Even if you're not into pussy, it was hard not to get an erection looking at the specific details he gave to every richly vein banger he ever drew.

"I thought about drawing some white boys taking it," Carlos threw out there one night, sketching at his drawing table.

"White boys? Taking it? Like bitches?" I questioned, not expecting something like that to come through his full lips after all the weeks we spent hanging out in his basement.

When he wasn't talking about his drawings, he was either talking about the last girl he fucked or when he was off to fuck another one.

"Yeah," Carlos said gruffly. "I don't know about you, but I couldn't get off on some other dude breaking dick off in my girl. Hell, half the time I'm pissed about sharing my Becky with any of you motherfuckers! So I got a theory about those boys that get off on letting another dude screwing their girl."

"What's that?"

"They secretly wish they had those helium heels, too!"

I laughed.

"You know I'm telling the truth, dawg," he continued, laughing.

"I hear you talking about drawing a dude getting fucked by another dude. Have you ever done that shit? Since you yourself said before that you get your inspiration from life."

"Oh hell-l-l no," Carlos shook his head, "one hundred percent wussy for pussy! The closest I ever came to letting one of those small dick beaters come to my dick is letting them suck me off. That ain't really gay. I mean, he's gay for taking another dude right in his mouth, but it just everyday tonsil work for me!"

"I heard that."

I wasn't expecting that just a few short days later that while I was hanging out in Carlos's basement that a blast from my past would come skipping down the stairs. As odd as it may sound, I wasn't all that shocked to see Rasool. Just a little thrown that he looked less like the Gulf War vet I remembered and more like a buffed out Rastafarian with his dreads pouring down his back.

"I think you remember my cousin," Carlos spat, and then followed up by pointing over to the stereo equipment in the corner that he was there to pick up.

There wasn't much we could say to each other without giving our story away, given that his crotch was shameless bulging like crazy. But he did manage to slip me a business card with his new cell phone number written on the back.

I knew I was playing with fire when I gave him a ring, but I reasoned that it had been forever since the last time I got down. Plus, it eliminated the hunt of if he or didn't he, like with Carlos. But, unlike the handful of times we hooked up before at his loft, he was bolder than bold showing up at my door in nothing on but some dazzling white briefs with this gigantic dick print straining underneath the elastic band.

"I think the two of you've met." He said arrogantly handsome.

"Yeah," I said, reaching out to touch the thing that made my life so complicated.

He pulled me in and closed the door behind me.

Even though his dick had always been a selling point with me, in the brief seconds he made it over to the bed, I nearly forgot about how incredible his body was, especially the back of his arms.

"Get to it, baby," Rasool said in a voice unlike his, very authoritatively, with his hands on his hardened V-shape waist.

I dropped to my knees, pulling his underwear down along the way. I learned long time ago that with a man like Rasool, I couldn't just cup his musky dick in my hand. No. I had to palm his big curvaceous ass and guide his big tool in with nothing more than my mouth. Because I took good care of him like this, he didn't grow mannishly heated by going for my head and trying to fuck my face.

"Get at it like a lollipop, son," he chided in his old hood dialect. "Like a lol-li-pop!"

He was speaking in tongues by the time I had him down my throat, his wild pubes tickling my nose and his low-hanging balls slinging against my chin, threatening to bust a nutt in my mouth at any moment when I was overcome by this strange feeling that someone was standing right behind me. Because I didn't hear anything to make me feel as if someone was actually behind me, I kept on sucking him off. It was just my imagination, I reasoned at best. But then, Rasool grabbed my head, putting his hands over both of my ears, and started slow-fucking my face like it was some fuck toy he'd just discovered.

"Oh, damn, son, I forgot you had that mouth made for gulping dick." Rasool said, as I felt his words vibrate through my smashed head. "Ah, shit!"

Rasool rode my mouth for a couple of more minutes and then out of nowhere, he just held my face steady before taking a few hard lunges and gasped, "Chug your man down, bitch!"

His dick was already down my throat, but he felt the need to ram it further in as if his hot load needed a direct route to my stomach.

I was screaming and gagging all at once, trying to pull off of him. But he wasn't ready to let me go, as it felt like I was guzzling a gallon down my weak little throat.

I felt ruined and done after that, rushed with the logic Carlos used to describe a faggot, mainly in the way I swallowed Rasool off like a baby to titty milk. But I couldn't even enjoy the confusing guilt of the moment as I felt a pair of gruff hands sliding my pants off my ass.

"What the fuck?" I heaved at a whisper after Rasool let go of my head, trying to look over my shoulder.

"You remember my cousin Carlos, right?" Rasool bragged. "I thought you might want to show him a good time, too."

I was so exhausted from the face-fucking that I couldn't even look back at him more or less move away from tightened grip he had on my waist.

"Don't be like that, kid. You know that I'll put it on you right … seeing that we're boys and shit." Carlos assured me, jokingly.

I let out a groan from my sore jaw as I heard something squirt out of a tube and some cold glob hit my exposed crack. I must've been open and wet from the blowjob I gave because Carlos fingered me with the lube with absolutely no problem, like I had just finishing up a down-home fuck. And when he went to push in with his eleven-inch monster, amazingly I took him in like a pro, finding the energy to sluggishly throw it back at him, so he could get the rest of it in.

"I didn't know you liked it like that, kid." Carlos heaved movingly, sliding the rest of his manly thickness into my stiff chute.

I gasped in pain. The pressure was head-busting ridiculous with water springing from my eyes.

Rasool responded, looking coldly in my eyes. "I told you Clay, here, was a pussy boy. He moaned like a little bitch the first time I put the pipe up in him."

As if my timing couldn't have been any worst, I let out one of those uncontainable groans followed by a series of terrifying body tremors, much like some of those white girls we double fuck in the same hole. His dick was beating up my prostate, and I was doing everything in my power from keeping my balls from draining out beneath me. But just the same, he was killing me with all these inching strokes, trying to stretch me out with his fat meat, so he could eventually go for rock bottom. Easing in and easing out, pushing and pulling, grunting and groaning because the tightness of my ass felt quite good to him.

"I told you that was some good ass. But if you want to get it in, you got to get in control of it, cuz. You got to break the seal off of ass like that like an unopened bottle top." Rasool coached with Carlos grunting.

After awhile, Carlos was fully fucking me, and my sore ass was being burned because of it, gutting my insides out.

"If I known this ass was like this I would've came for it long time ago." Carlos huffed, ramming his brick hard dick up in me. "Think about all those nights we could've had together. The fun we could've had fucking just like this in my basement! A black boy could've taken just as easy as a white boy!"

I think we both got lost in the sensation, two straight dudes coming together and enjoying each other like this after all this time. He was thinking back to when we started hanging out, but I was on another plane thinking about the fun we could've had all those years ago, regretting that his cousin, not him, was my not my first.

"You gonna take my load, dawg," Carlos pumped harder, almost fiendishly by then.

"Yeah," I huffed, getting the wind knocked out of me.

"I can't hear you, dawg. You gonna take my load?"

"Yeah, man … damn," I whined, afraid that I was so open by his fucking that his balls was starting to go in.

"You want me to put my babies up in that womb? Impregnate that hungry hole? Huh? Tell me what you want to do, kid!"

"I want you to do what you do, C." I mumbled.

"You want Big C to fuck that kid's pussy good, don't you?"

"Yes," I cried aloud, letting my bitched-out pleasure betray my once-formidable manhood.

"You want me to beat it up, rip that boy-pussy wide open, don't you?"

I couldn't find the energy to say anything else. I just let out moans and groans to let him know that I was with him however he wanted to get in.

"I'm gonna come in that good-ass pussy, bitch. I'm gonna fill you up with these motherfucking babies, kid. You gonna be that good bitch for me from here on out! Right?!?!" Carlos went in hard like a rabid fiend, putting the screws to my already-sore butt cheeks. Next thing I knew, he was deeper in my ass than he was before, offering no apologies, pushed back against my waist, and pulled harder back in, shouting, "Take it like a bitch, punk! Take my cum up in your pussy, bitch! Yeah, bitch! Uhhhnnnnggggh!"

To say Carlos shot a load up my ass would be understatement. Dude exploded in my ass and flooded it with hot cum. And with my insides feeling full because of it, it forced me to bust my own nutt right there on the floor, hands free. And if that wasn't enough, when he went to pull his dick out of my ass and the cum started gushing out of me like a broken egg over my balls, forcing me to shoot another load as if the first one didn't count. Again, hands free.

They didn't bitch me out too bad after that. They just made a few badly timed jokes at my expense, but oddly enough kept it very professional the handful of times we made a go of the sex thing after that.

The three of us were hanging out in Carlos's basement one night when I noticed that the two cousins were shooting glances at each other and then back at me relaxing on the couch. It wasn't that I wasn't above serving them up some, but it seemed that they started to pin me as star ho in our little arrangement.

"I love my pussy, too," I said grabbing my dick, reminding the two of them that I still had one.

A nice big one at that.

So I made the plea that we call up our boy and see if he could get us a line on some nasty girl that was willing to do all three of us. To my surprise, our boy didn't just get a bite, he cast a net and caught plenty of fish that wanted to party with a bunch of roughnecks from around the way.

A few hours later, we converted Carlos's studio basement into a dimly-lit party room full of blacks and blondes. Many of the guys were from around our old neighborhood and most of the girls were the suburban desperate housewives types that were in need of a little fun. Obviously coming from a middle-class neighborhood, most of the men there weren't roughnecks in the stereotypical Hollywood sense, it was a nice mixture of men, some educated with white-collared jobs and others worked blue-collared ones. I don't think that really mattered to the girls on the hunt for some seasoned black sausage.

After people started pairing off, some going elsewhere while others got it in and bounced, the three of us found ourselves sitting on the sofa smoking bud and getting sucked off by three white girls. I was feeling especially proud since my girl looked like one of those generic big-breasted porn stars.

Then, out of nowhere, I felt something crawl up my asshole as she was giving me a blowjob, only to discover that it was her finger. I didn't want to bring any unwanted attention to myself and the way she hooked to my prostate just so I just left at, "You're going to make me come real quick like that."

So she kept on and on. No problem. But then she went from tonguing my balls to tonguing the spot where my ass crack started to form. I tried stopping her, but she kept on anyway. The purple haze started to get the best of me, and I felt a pair of hands grab each of my legs holding them up some kind of way. I must've dozed off for a second because when I came to I still felt that tongue in my ass and some hands grabbing my legs. This time though I had some sleeping dick swinging lazily slapping me in my face.

"Put in your mouth," the voice boomed over my head. "Suck it like a lollipop."

And while my head wasn't there because of the weed and my senses telling me to get out of there, I stupidly fished for the elusive head with my lips. The room erupted in roar, with the faceless man in front of me telling the room that a man that liked his ass played with wasn't too far away from sucking a dick.

"Go ahead. Suck my dick." The man continued.

I was torn between wanting to and not wanting to, and in the last minute, I decided to go for it forgetting that others were in the room that quickly reminded me of their presence by the roar and laughter erupting in the room.

I probably put four of five more dicks in my mouth after that, getting them wet and nothing more given that my coordination wasn't focused enough to stay on point, to blow them all off.

"What that ass do, folk?" I heard a familiar voice ask from behind a man that I had my lips wrapped around.

"That ass is nice, man ... just like pussy." Carlos confirmed.

"Like pussy?"

"Like pussy with super-duper vice grip." Carlos laughed.

"We'll see about that." Decker, the familiar voice and one of the heads of my old robbing crew, said, lifting one of my legs up and jamming a finger up in there.

I wanted to tell him to stop, but in no time flat, with a slimy dick, he just shoved his way into my closed up hole. There was nothing I could do about the assault, given that the man standing in front of me stopped me from pushing him away. But even Decker had to get him off of me to get a better look.

"I've been wanting to fuck your lame ass for a long time. Back when you were in high school carrying yourself up to

Rally's during your lunch time." Decker, eight years older than I, growled in my ear.

He smelled of blunts, but surprised me when he began driving his tongue past my lips and started exploring my mouth, palming my waist down to my ass, and giving me the soulful fuck I needed to get into it.

That turned out to be a good thing since there were so many others that wanted a crack at my ass, starting with other guys my age from my neighborhood and robbing crew to older married guys that I looked at from afar growing up, leaving me loose with grease and cum.

I was in and out of my high, craving the munchies badly to remembering every face of every man that I needed to be ashamed to hang my head high around from here on out. So I tried hard to make the most of every dick when I was conscious.

I don't know which came first, being dragged to another room before the random fucking or after, but at any rate I was laid out on some bed taking a few dudes before I found my way onto the floor and onto my knees.

I don't remember anybody else being in that room except Carlos. But he was standing there right in front of me with his dick hanging out, looking for a blowjob. I tried to refuse. It wasn't that I was trying to act like I hadn't done it before as I was simply exhausted from my ass being so well used.

He didn't care one way or the other.

He just plugged my mouth, and like a good boy I licked it like a lollipop, trying to imagine that it was one of those weed-tasting ones they sold at the gas station. I was sucking, and he was fucking my face, making sure that I had the focus that I didn't have before. Then out of nowhere, this warm stuff started consistently spraying into my mouth. I took me a second to figure out that it was piss, and I started spitting that shit out. He wasn't having any of that, gagging his dick further down my throat.

"I know you're not trying to back off of this shit." Carlos said, fucking my face. "Unlike nutt, piss is sterile, and as much cum you'd taken tonight, you need all the sterilization you can get!"

He took another shot of piss in my mouth.

"Drink up, bitch," he stormed. "I know you're thirsty."

Carlos pumped away, and I don't know, something got into me, and I drank that shit up like it was liquor. I was thirsty for every drop. He was laughing at me, and I was sucking him like sucking dick was something new to me and I loved it. As I was gobbling his dick down like it was the last edible thing on earth, I felt him shoot in my mouth, and I let it ease down my throat like the medicine from a good cough drop, it was nasty but good for me.

"I don't have to tell you to swallow that shit good. Just take it down slow, just like a lollipop."

MOOKIE
By R. Talent

Your freaky ass would, I thought.

I was trying hard to suppress my need to laugh with a huge smile plastered across my face. It was funny and sexy as hell at the same time.

His dick was proud and drooling like crazy arching its way back toward the rigid rippling effect that was his stomach. One could argue that he was excited because he was looking up at me and the sleeping monster between my legs that treated him so well. But I knew better than that. That was more like icing on the cake in comparison to what I was doing to him right then.

It started out as one of those Friday nights between two close friends, Mookie and I, where we was ready to get our party and bullshit on, donned in our flyest gear. We made our rounds, shot some game, and upped the ante almost every half-hour until we struck out. Striking out at a time when we both needed to be broken off something good. Afterwards, we rolled over to a sex party that proved not to be the jump-off like it was the week before. Even the dude that was collecting the money at the door knew what was up and gave us a refund and then some for simply coming out. Next came our stroll over to the late night diner, where Mookie and I flirted with this waiter that was down for pulling a train for the two of us. But, as luck would have it, he wasn't due to come off the clock for at least another six hours. We were destined to save our night, but the only thing we did was head back to the crib and tear up a bottle of 150 proof and some purple haze.

We drank and talked, drank and bullshitted, talked and partied, and drank some more. We drank like we were fish in the sea, feeling good and carefree. Somewhere along the way, I fetched Mookie to the kitchen to microwave some Hot Pockets, and he came back with some bananas talking about we needed our potassium. I tried yelling him back into the kitchen to do what I told him to do. All Mookie wanted to do was eat his banana; skin first ... before he came to and eventually peeled it off. He ate it in such a seductive manner that it made me regret not sticking with the first piece I hooked earlier that night. But no, I thought that the redbone was better looking than he, and that the sunshine yellow dude was better looking than the redbone, and I simply lucked out on everybody. I said out loud that I was horny. Mookie told me that he was at a crossroads, between us, real talk. Mookie wanted to get fucked but never got fucked before, so he really didn't know if he really wanted to go through with it in the first place.

An opening, all I needed was an opening. And being that we were boyz, I knew what to use and how to use it to my advantage. Besides, what stranger can do you better than your homeboy? He knew I could fuck. Mookie had been right there beside me running those old-fashioned Chattanooga choo-choos on those young bucks with those hungry watering holes famished for our well-fed sea serpents. Mookie knew I could fuck, but knew that he didn't want my kind of fucking. Not at my usual ravenous tempo that could make ol' Bobby Blake look like a softy.

"We're friends, not fuck buddies." I cajoled him carefully, adding that "those other bitches we usually find are in heat and need a freak that will leave them comatose after the fact. Man, I know you ain't like that! You're my boy, nah-mean?"

So I took him in the back and hammered him out. He took my third leg like a trooper. He wasn't a virgin like he said, though. Not a true, genuine never-had-his-cherry-popped virgin. The way his hole gripped it and talked back I knew that it had been a few years since he got the bottom knocked out of his bumbling brown ass. Toward the middle and end of it though, Mookie was riding it like a ten-speed, never losing his incredible stride.

Mookie and I took it back to the living room and got back to the liquor and weed an hour before sunrise. I sprawled out on the sofa leaving him nowhere to sit, other than to lie at my feet on the rugged floor.

It started off by accident, with me staring at the ceiling and moving my feet towards the floor. Mookie didn't say anything and neither did I. I just felt the warmness of his chest and stomach on underneath my wide heavy foot. It was heaven to be high, terrible to be drunk, and empty to be spent. And yet, to be like that all at the same time with the cool air rolling over our naked bodies was just the median I needed. I happened to look down, looking at a friend looking back at me as if he couldn't believe what we had just done back there in that bedroom. I let Mookie know that he wasn't just another piece of ass by plucking his nipples with my long toes, nice and slow.

We didn't say another word to each other. We just let the mood in the room talk for us, occasionally sharing glances that spoke volumes over mere words. I got lost in the possibilities of us, or at least the next time we can do what we did again. I swept my other foot over his torso, and I listened to him playful whine that my foot was cold as he was caressing it warmly in his hand. I did him a favor and tucked my other foot back under my leg and the sofa to try and warm it up as well.

Mookie inhaled deeply as I used my cold foot to pluck at his nipples once more. I caught his dick sleepily drifting up from his lap. With the last blunt in my mouth, I decided to share with my friend this one last thing. I put it in between my big toe and the one next to it and coast it over his mouth, his lips, and instructed him to take a toke.

He did, nice and very slowly with my toes and the ball of my foot pressed against his soft lips like the kiss we never truly shared.

DREAM OF A PLAYER
By Aaron Cromwell

Pete had the best job he could ever wish for. The pay was unimpressive, the hours were long and the kid's boss could be a real jerk sometimes. But with the work came perks in the form of mostly black drop-dead sexy, virulent men. Despite this, the perks were never the reason the twenty-four-year-old loved his job. Pete had long been a football fanatic, and he deeply enjoyed using physical therapy to help people.

Most of the men he worked with were a pleasure to view, but he never had difficulty being perfectly professional with them at all times – that is, until he encountered Derrick Wallace. He was an incredible physical specimen, described by some NFL analysts as a genetic freak because of his outstanding measurables, a term reserved for only the most impressive athletes. Coming out of college, team scouts believed Derrick had limitless potential, but due to off-the-field issues, he wasn't selected until late in the second round of the draft.

Derrick's physique was as incredibly constructed for pleasure as it was for athletics. Thick, full dreads came down to his neck, framing a square-jawed face that reflected his toughness. Body ink decorated his dark skin from his neck to his legs, adding to the intimidating presence the young man was known for, the other element Pete found so attractive.

Derrick had been in trouble as far back as high school, and once he became a star college football player, his non-football issues were widely publicized. Derrick had little family or support system, and it would have been easy to degenerate into a life of crime, but instead, he poured his heart and soul into the game he loved.

But while that love provided Derrick a bright future, another love that he kept hidden caused him great stress. Derrick believed he had to make a choice between being gay and following his dream of playing in the NFL. He didn't regret his choice, but the denial of his love was a heavy burden, which drove him to act out. Along with other problems, he was frequently getting into fights with teammates over often trivial disputes, the very reason he was cut from his last team.

In addition to the amazing body, deep gravelly voice, masculine attitude and his sexy swagger, there was something about Derrick that was completely irresistible to Pete – something none of the other players had. From the moment Pete met the third-year safety, he knew working with this man would be a difficult challenge. Their relationship began smoothly, but it was less than a month later that the incident occurred.

"Good morning," Pete greeted Derrick as he reclined on the therapy bed. The usually friendly player was cold and silent in response. Pete was powdering Derrick's leg in preparation for his early morning treatment.

In front of the other trainers and players in the room, for everyone to hear, Derrick growled, "You fuckin' faggot," shoving Pete violently to the ground.

After Derrick stormed out of the room, a couple others came to Pete's aid, asking him if he was all right. Though it was a shock to the people there, nothing much came of the incident. It was exactly the kind of volatility people expected from Derrick.

Pete sighed exhaustedly when the day was finally over, and he could go home. It was dark and quiet as he left the facility.

Pete was shocked to see Derrick waiting for him outside. Pete immediately began trembling as he backed away with tears welling in his eyes. "Oh, god," his voice quivered with fear. "Please, man, p-please don't hurt me. Please, I'm sorry ..."

"No, look," Derrick interrupted as he moved forward. "I'm sorry, okay? I just came to apologize. I didn't mean to go off on you like that." Derrick paused with a sigh as he explained, "I don't even know why I did. I knew you were gay soon as we met."

"No! No, I swear I'm not gay!"

Derrick smirked at him and said, "It's okay, dude, I don't care."

"I'm really not! I swear I'm ..."

Derrick grinned at the unconvincing protests. "All right, man, whatever. I've just been really stressed out lately. I ... It's hard to explain, but I'm sorry."

After a pause, Pete offered, "I'm sorry."

"Not your fault," he said with a smile. "We good?" Derrick held up his hand to Pete.

Pete hesitated for a moment, but Derrick's sincerity won him over. "Yeah," he answered as they wrapped hands and bumped shoulders. "We're good."

"Look, I was thinkin', lemme make it up to you somehow. You wanna come back to my place and keep me company? Help me relieve some stress? Maybe we could play Madden or something."

"No, that's okay, you don't have to."

"I know I don't have to, but I want to, man."

Pete forced a smile to show appreciation, but he was still nervous. "It's really all right. I mean, I forgive you and all."

"Please though? Come on, I could use the company."

Pete had fantasized of spending time with Derrick since they met, but under the circumstances, he wasn't so sure he wanted to go through with it. He took a breath as he hesitated, wanting to just forget the whole day and in some way too embarrassed to be around Derrick. In the end, he couldn't resist Derrick's winning smile. "I guess ... All right," Pete said shyly.

Derrick smiled as he led the way to his car, walking slowly enough to keep the still very nervous Pete at his side. On the way to his home, Derrick was talkative like he typically was, trying to be friendly, and Pete engaged in the conversation as best as he could considering how uncomfortable he still felt.

Once inside Derrick's sizable but plainly decorated house, they sat on the couch and Derrick started a game of Madden. As the game loaded, Pete couldn't resist admiring the player's muscled body, but quickly looked away when Derrick noticed him.

"Sorry!" Pete murmured as he turned red with embarrassment that he'd been caught making the same mistake for the second time in one day.

Derrick just laughed and said, "Hey, I told you it's okay. I don't mind you lookin'. It's actually flattering." Pete still wouldn't face him, so he decided to get the nervous kid's attention another way. Derrick stood up in front of Pete and took off his shirt, flexing his arms and chest, teasing Pete who looked up only briefly at the amazing sight. Derrick laughed at his own antics and sat down again next to Pete.

Derrick smiled and asked, "You like what you see?" Pete was still too nervous to answer but it was obvious he was very attracted. "You want to touch?"

Pete looked into Derrick's eyes to see if he was actually serious, and though it appeared he was, Pete was paralyzed with both excitement and nervousness.

Derrick's smile showed off his perfect white teeth as he took Pete's hand and pressed it against his right bicep. Pete looked at what he was touching as Derrick moved the younger guy's hand up and down. After a few moments, Pete felt comfortable enough to lightly squeeze the powerful muscle in his hand.

As soon as he did, Derrick forcefully pushed Pete down onto his back on the couch, causing Pete to cry out in fear for a moment before Derrick's mouth covered his own with a heated, rough kiss. Pete's scream turned into a moan as his body relaxed in submission to Derrick's power.

Pete looked at Derrick to confirm this was real, which the intensity of his dark eyes proved. As Derrick's hands moved possessively over the submissive body, Pete held on to the hard muscle-packed man on top of him. Derrick kissed and lightly bit at Pete's lips, face, neck and ears as Pete breathed harder and harder with lust for the sexy beast on top of him.

After a few minutes of this passionate kissing, Derrick looked down into Pete's eyes and asked, "You wanna suck me?"

With disbelief at his great luck, Pete nodded vigorously at the offer. Derrick smiled in return and lay back with his legs outstretched on the couch. He grabbed at the full package in his jeans and said to Pete, "Come get some."

Pete couldn't get his face in Derrick's lap quickly enough, eager to kiss and caress the growing bulge. "Take it out," Derrick told him.

Obediently, he unzipped the jeans and pulled them down around his muscular tight ass and thick thighs, followed by his form-fitting underwear. Once he'd gotten Derrick completely naked, Pete dived back down to meet the oversized cock and balls. Pete took a moment to process how lucky he was to have the opportunity to please such an awesome man. He massaged the large balls as his mouth kissed then enveloped the head of Derrick's thick and now very hard dick.

Pete moaned as he sucked Derrick, who used a hand in Pete's hair to set a steady rhythm to the head he was getting. Pete loved sucking that massive, veiny black dick, but he was even more excited about the pleasure he was giving Derrick. He encouraged his cocksucker, saying things like, "Aw yeah, that feels so good," and, "Mm, just like that."

Massaging Derrick's large balls and muscular thighs as he sucked harder, Pete went down as far as he could on the thick dick and stroked the rest with his hand. This was Pete's dream come true, and he couldn't ask for anything better than hearing the man he had a hopeless crush on moaning with pleasure.

Derrick was thrilled with this treatment, having always wanted a blowjob from a guy, and now that he was getting it from a cute guy who was just his type, he was ready to come within minutes. When he did, Pete happily swallowed it all and laid his head in Derrick's lap as he savored the sweet cum.

Derrick absently stroked Pete's head as he voiced his appreciation, "Damn, Pete, you suck real good." Pete responded with a moan and lingering kisses to Derrick's crotch. "You love it, too, huh? You ready for some more fun?" Derrick asked.

He looked up at the man and smiled, feeling completely relaxed, as he nodded in agreement, wondering what would come next.

"Come on." The pair stood and with his hands on Pete's hips and his torso pressed against Pete's back, Derrick guided him to his bedroom. Once inside, Derrick's hot mouth kissed and licked Pete's ears and neck while his hands worked on taking off Pete's jeans then shirt.

Nervously, Pete asked, "You're gonna fuck me?"

"Oh yes," Derrick whispered sexily into Pete's ear. "And I know you want it," he said playfully as he grinded against Pete's ass.

Derrick pushed Pete forward to lie on his stomach on the king-sized bed, then knelt over the smooth white bubble butt, squeezing it firmly with both hands. Derrick gave it one good smack before reaching for the lube in the drawer, laying his hot body over Pete's as he did so.

Back on his knees, Derrick spread Pete's cheeks and poked with his middle finger at the tight pink pucker, teasing it gently, making Pete's whole body shiver with tickles of pleasure and his dick harden to full stiffness.

Derrick smacked Pete's butt with his dick, increasing the anticipation for both of them. Pete looked back over his shoulder and saw Derrick smiling as he played with Pete's ass, like a kid playing with a new toy.

As Pete's pleasure from the foreplay increased, his body began to respond on its own accord. He was pushing his ass back for more attention, begging to be touched and fucked. Derrick was eager to oblige the request. With one hand, he lubed his fully erect and throbbing ten-inch dick, and with the other, he fingered Pete, spreading the lube thoroughly. Pete would have benefited from more stretching, but Derrick was excited and wanted to get in the white ass below him immediately.

Pressing one hand against Pete's back, Derrick lined his dick up to the tight hole and pushed the thick head in firmly. Pete arched his back up and fought the urge to get away from the painfully invading member.

Derrick moaned loud and deep as he inched farther into Pete. "Damn, so tight!"

Pete tried hard to bear the pain, but as another inch forced its way inside, he resisted, putting a hand back to push against Derrick's stomach and screamed out, "God, it hurts!"

Derrick pushed the pained bottom boy back down to the bed and pinned his arm against his back, loading his ass with more dick. He insistently stretched Pete's hole as he writhed beneath Derrick, trying to adjust. "Fuck! This ass loves my dick!"

Pete's body heated up from the pain, his face sweating and turning bright red. "Ouch! Derrick!"

"Oh yeah!" Derrick yelled. "Say my name!" Pete groaned and tried to crawl away, but Derrick refused his escape. "Where ya goin'?" he teased as he dragged Pete back underneath him. "What's my name, bitch?" Derrick jabbed his dick at an angle, making Pete feel a sharper pain, punctuating his demand. "Say it!"

"Derrick!"

"Yeah!" he shouted excitedly, thrusting hard, making Pete yelp.

Derrick fucked Pete with a steady well-paced rhythm and quickly sped up until his hips were loudly slapping Pete's butt twice per second, making him cry out repeatedly, "Ow, ow, ow!"

He bit down on a pillow to cope with the pain as Derrick worked hard at nailing Pete's ass to the bed. Pete's face was covered in sweat and colored red hot, while his eyes watered from the painful stretch in his ass. Finally, Pete couldn't take it anymore and begged for release, "Derrick, please stop! It's too much! It hurts too much! Please take it out for a second!"

Panting from the workout, Derrick slowed down and laid his body down firmly on top of Pete and gently assured him, "No, no, no. I got you, baby. Don't worry. I got you."

"Derrick, please no! It hurts so bad!" Pete whined as Derrick reached under him to rub his now soft penis. Derrick continued thrusting hard but now at a slower pace, and with the new angle he was suddenly grazing Pete's prostate roughly.

Derrick fucked Pete like that whose painful "Ow, ow, ow!" turned into a much more pleasurable "Oh, oh, oh!" Derrick seemed to instinctively know how to hit that spot inside of Pete that made his jaw drop open, his eyes roll into the back of his head, and his whole body quiver with sensation.

"See?" Derrick said. "I got you."

Pete gasped, "Oh yeah, man, you do! You do!" Pete's pain was still undeniable, but now it was accompanied by the intense electric tingles in his ass that radiated throughout his body.

"Say my name," Derrick's deep voice whispered into his bottom's ear as he stroked the white boy's now hardening cock while his other arm wrapped around Pete's head under his chin, his rock-like bicep flexing its power. "What's my name?"

"Mmm," Pete moaned as he answered, "Derrick."

"Yeah, there you go. Who's fucking you? Huh?"

"Derrick's fucking me."

"Who owns this ass, boy?"

The question alone inspired a blissful tingle in Pete's brain only matched by his following admission, "Derrick does. Derrick owns my ass."

Derrick reveled in the submission he'd coaxed out of the white boy under him. "Yeahhh," Derrick whispered, steadily fucking the ass he'd just claimed.

Pete loved this treatment, and his ass was pushing back for more of Derrick's big dick, now absolutely in love with its pounding inside of him.

The pain had subsided to the amazing feelings, both physical and emotional. Derrick was fucking Pete so good he was completely submerged in the sensations, oblivious to everything else. He just knew that he had a heavy 230 pounds of rock-hard black muscle on top of him and an equally hot, hard dick spearing his ass.

With his head firmly against Derrick's chest and shoulder, Pete soon climaxed from the hot fuck he was getting. As his hole spasmed tightly around Derrick's big black dick, the muscular, dominant top was pushed to his own orgasm, coming deep inside of Pete.

"Ahhh, fuck yeah!" Derrick shouted as he continued grinding his dick in Pete's ass. After his prolonged orgasm finally subsided, he let his entire bodyweight rest on top of Pete, holding him tight. With one arm still around Pete's neck and the other wrapped across his chest, he pressed his cheek against the side of Pete's head, staying as close to him as possible.

Though the bigger body weighed heavily on him, Pete would have been content to remain there for eternity. When

Derrick finally pulled himself out of the roughly fucked ass, he turned Pete over, so they could kiss passionately, which quickly had them both aroused again. Their love-making continued for hours, Pete getting fucked hard out of his mind at times, but always being dominated romantically.

Pete woke up the next morning to Derrick kissing his face. "You hungry?" Derrick asked. Pete nodded excitedly and scrambled to get his mouth on the huge dick resting between Derrick's legs.

Derrick gasped in surprise as he lay back and protested with an amused chuckle, "'Ey, Pete, I was talkin' about gettin' some food – Oh shit, that feels good!" After Derrick was done filling Pete's mouth with another load of cum, they stopped at McDonald's on their way back to work.

Two days later, it was the first game of the season – a big game for the team and a huge game for Derrick since he'd be playing in place of the regular starter who was injured.

Derrick was extremely confident in himself, and Pete was nervously excited for his big chance. Pete couldn't help being fascinated with how hot Derrick was in his uniform, and everyone in the stadium was fascinated by his performance. By the end of the game, he'd racked up 11 tackles, a pick-6 and a forced fumble. Derrick literally wowed the crowd with a hit on a receiver that an announcer called "vicious," arousing Pete even more for the amazing athlete.

It was during a post-game interview that Pete learned what motivated Derrick to play so well, his talent shining more than ever before.

"I just decided to be me, to trust my instincts, so I was the best I could be."

The Authors

AARON CROMWELL writes for fun and loves getting feedback with this being his first time being published, and he looks forward to many more opportunities. aaroncromwell@gmail.com; www.aaroncromwell.blogspot.com.

DANDY DIXON writes queer erotica, the illustrated *Horny Hill* series, and is a DJ in the San Francisco Bay Area. He's one of the last unicorns known to man. www.dandydixon.com.

DERRICK DELLA GIORGIA was born in Italy and currently lives between Manhattan and Rome. His work has been published in several anthologies and literary magazines. Visit him at www.derrickdellagiorgia.com.

DON MIKA lives in North Carolina. He loves to write, and can be reached at little_big_mann@yahoo.com.

DONALD WEBB has had stories published in numerous gay magazines and anthologies. He lives with his life-time partner in Victoria, BC. He is currently seeking a publisher for a completed mystery novel. andon402@shaw.ca.

EVAN GILBERT lives and works in Memphis, Tennessee.

JUNIOR has been writing since he was a very young child. He enjoys intelligent debates, and his hope for the future is to challenge the views of a stunted society. He is currently working on a novel that he intends to publish under his real name, as well as developing a script and soliciting funds to produce a short film.

LANDON DIXON'S stories have been published in numerous magazines and anthologies, many of which are published by STARbooks Press.

LOGAN ZACHARY (loganzachary2002@yahoo.com) is an author of mysteries, short stories, and over forty erotica stories, living in Minneapolis with his partner, Paul, and his dog, Ripley, who runs the house. www.loganzacharydicklit.com.

R. TALENT is a freelance writer who drives his big-rig and plays poker whenever he isn't bothering his partner, Diesel King, about throwing a freaky third or a fourth into their cell of a relationship. He is a frequent contributor to STARBooks Press in over ten anthologies and is still working on his long-awaited debut novel.

R. W. CLINGER has numerous short stories and three novels available from STARbooks Press. R. W. is currently at work on new gay novel.

RAWIYA is a happily married mother of two who's had seven short works published. http://rawiyaserotica.blogspot.com.

The Editor

MARCUS ANTHONY is a writer and editor, residing in Newport News, Virginia. He is the epitome of tall, dark and delicious.

ng any underwear. "Excuse me," I said, having a hard time looking
ed by that bulge in his crotch, "but don't I know you?" "Maybe," h
of t   bout a m
Ray   God, you
ser?   in?" he as
"Lik   s stronges
ody   e on Gree
he l   I ever sa
to t   any ideas?
king   e same
coul   ery long t
rac   ne swell.
with   e in store
go   behind so
ee   in public
" he   vent to the
cy.   grabbed
d. I
raci   t, so firm
t, ha
n m   bing dick
g, I   n cock, be
ound of unzipping filled the small space. I don't know who's hand
before I knew it, I had his rod in my hand, and mine was in his. ""
do?" he asked, his tone challenging. I knew exactly, and sank to m

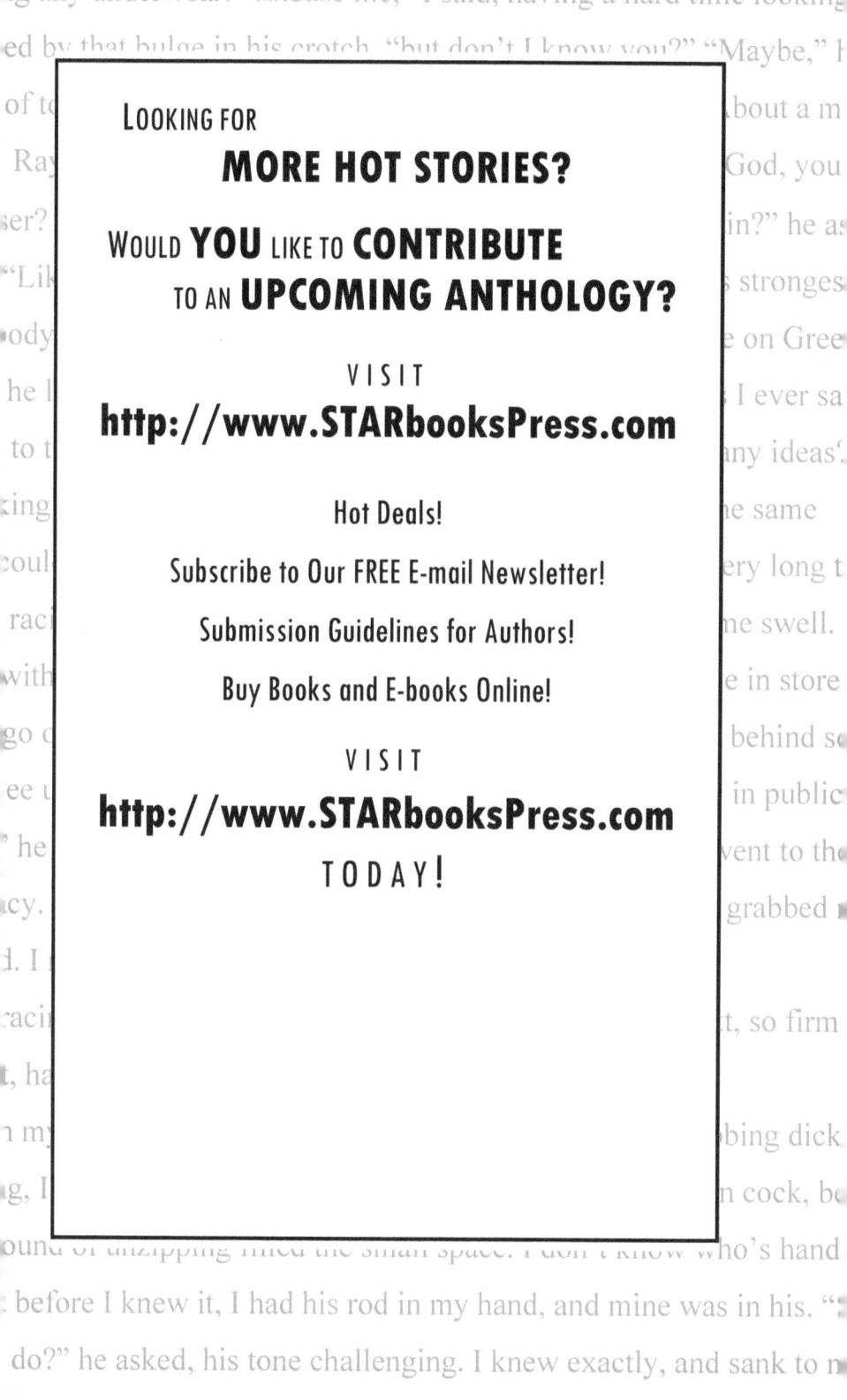

www.ingramcontent.com/pod-product-compliance
Lightning Source LLC
Chambersburg PA
CBHW020839260626
47169CB00003B/1061